# RAVEN'S NEST

## A CONSPIRACY OF RAVENS BOOK FOUR

# SHELBY LEE

# *table of contents*

# *author's note*

Raven's Nest is a dark, romantic suspense novel that contains triggering situations. It is a why choose novel, meaning our heroine does not ever have to choose between our three heroes. This book is intended for mature audiences 18+ and contains the word 'fuck' probably far too many times.

For a full content warning list, please visit:
   http://www.authorshelbylee.com

*My loving husband,*
*Thank you for supporting me on this wild journey and being my*
*own why choose situation... only with less dicks.*
*You're everything to me, and this series wouldn't be here without*
*you.*

# *pierce*

Bright light streams through the open window. It burns my bare skin more than the heat River's body is giving off at my side. He rolls over and wraps his arm around my middle, then smashes his face into my chest. I snort and shake my head as I wind my fingers through his hair, massage his scalp and take a deep breath.

We're all fucking alive.

That's what matters right now.

The night without Raven was weird, but I knew she needed her space. She needed to take a breath without us hovering over her. We should have given her a dose of the anti-drug, but what drove us to do it without her was fear.

Fear of the unknown.

Hell, even fear of the things we do know.

It's a risk, making an antidrug in a crazed man's basement, but it's better than being dosed with its counterpart. It hasn't killed us yet, and Rapture has killed in minutes.

I'll beg for her forgiveness for the end of time, because we have an actual shot at that now.

"Move the fuck over," Phoenix grumbles. He shoves me in the side and groans when River reaches out and smacks him. "Why the hell did we share the bed if she's not here?"

"Better get used to life like this, Nixy boy." River's voice is gruff, and the sound does things to me. "Good morning to you too, Pierce."

I slap a hand over my face and sigh. "We should all apologize at the same time... right?"

"Probably best to present a united front." River smacks a kiss to my chest and sits up with a yawn.

My attraction and love for him has only grown this past week and a half, and I realize I still have a lot of growing to do. A lot of accepting of him and me. The world has pushed me down so fucking much that I can't accept the good things right in front of my face.

A knock at the door draws all three of our attention.

"You think that's her?" River asks. He doesn't wait for us to answer, simply shoots to his feet, adjusts his dick in his boxers, and strides right up to the door. "Good morning, RaeRae. I knew it wouldn't take a big grovel fest to—oh! Uh. Morning, Tris." He sticks his head out, then stands straight. "What's up?"

"I... should have said something last night... but you guys were all angry and..." Tris looks down at her feet, and River pulls her in for a hug.

"Hey, we can help with whatever's going on. Just tell us. Where's Rae?"

"Well... that's the thing... she's... she's gone."

"What the fuck do you mean, *she's gone?*" I snap, shooting to my feet and rushing toward them.

"Pierce," Phoenix calls.

But fuck him.

I push past a panicking River and crying Tris, and rush down the hall, toward the door I was at only hours before, begging the woman I love to forgive me for protecting her.

*Would she really leave? Just like that?*

"Raven!" I yell. "Raven, I'm coming in there. You can be mad all you want, but I'm coming in."

"Pierce, she's—"

I turn my glare on Tris and shake my head before turning back to the room. With my heart hammering in my chest, and nausea settling in my gut, I grab the handle, twist, and swing the door wide open.

"What the fuck?" Phoenix asks as he walks inside behind me.

She's not on the bed... under it... in the closet...

"Where the hell is she?" I shout, tossing a pillow at the wall and pinning Tris with another sharp glare. "When did she leave?"

"Last night... she—"

"She left last fucking night? Why the hell didn't you come get one of us?" Our footsteps echo in the hallway and down the stairs as I search for her.

I sprint into the basement.

Maybe she went down there. Curious. In search of one of us?

Not here.

River yells at me to slow down when I burst through the back door and begin tossing everything around.

It's ridiculous to think I'd find her under a lounge chair, but I'd rather be ridiculous than not search everywhere.

When I rush back toward the tree line, I take note of the rest of Lance's team searching for Raven there, and I spin back around.

They'd have found her by now.

Right?

I keep searching for my best friend. The love of my life.

High.

Low.

Anywhere.

Everywhere.

Only to find her... nowhere.

"Fuck!" I yell into the fucking void because no one else is listening, that's for sure.

"I didn't mean to keep it from you..." Tris mutters as I enter the house again. She's looking at Phoenix, yet her gaze keeps landing on the window where we can see Lance's car. "I was..."

"A shiny new toy distracted you, and you let my girl get the fuck away!" I shout.

"Pierce," River snaps, both his voice and his fingers. He pins me with a glare and I shrink in on myself for a moment as our eyes meet. "Breathe. Sit the fuck down. You're not doing anyone any good by being an asshole."

I want to argue, but when I start to, he grips me by the shoulder and forces me to sit down at the table.

Mark finally makes his way down the stairs and looks around at everyone in a panic, a Glock held firmly in his hand as he takes stock of the situation. When he sees Tris in tears and me being held down, he pins me with a dangerous expression. "What the hell have you done to my daughter?"

I scoff, but River squeezes my shoulder hard enough I wince and keep my mouth shut.

"Apologies, Mark," Phoenix says. He grabs a cup of coffee like it's another fucking day in paradise, but I see his knuckles as they turn white.

"Explain," Mark says as he sits down beside his crying daughter.

"Nope," River grits out in my ear. He sits next to me and passes me a cup of coffee once Phoenix makes it. "Not your fucking turn, Jackson."

I growl in return, but keep my mouth shut except for drinking caffeine. I'll need it to make a plan to find my girl. She may think she can leave, but she doesn't recognize how possessive I really am over her.

"Raven's gone," Phoenix says as he sits down.

Too fucking casual.

My entire body is shaking with tension and he's sitting there like it's a fucking happy Sunday morning.

"Gone?" Mark asks. He looks at his daughter, then back at us. "What do you mean?"

"That's as much as I have," Phoenix says. "I'd appreciate it if you told us what you know, Tris."

"She got up in the middle of the night and grabbed the last dose of the anti-drug. She took it and—"

"She fucking took it?" A deep breath is not enough to contain the anger, but with River holding me down, I can't do shit. "She just fucking took the goddamn thing after we explicitly told her—"

"Our problem, Pierce," Phoenix snarls, "is that you keep telling her shit. It's a mutual fucking relationship. She's on our level. Hell, if anything, we're far below hers." He stands and chugs the rest of his coffee before tossing the mug in the sink.

Tris jumps when it shatters.

Phoenix takes a deep breath and braces his hands on the counter as he stares out the window. "I'm going to text Lance. River?"

Gray eyes peer up from the table, but he remains stoic.

"Get him under control. Meet me outside."

River nods and yanks me to a stand. He gives no fucks when the table scratches my stomach, nor when I damn near break an ankle while he drags me up the stairs by the wrist.

"What the—"

He slams me against the wall beside the door in our room, and I wince. His glare makes me feel two inches tall, and when he collars my throat and squeezes just enough to threaten my airway, all my thoughts come to a standstill.

Neither of us can say a word without pissing the other off, and no one's popping a boner anytime soon, so we simply stare until our breathing calms and the threat of hurting one another physically or emotionally dies down.

"You good?" he asks once I'm no longer balling my hands into fists.

I nod, and he releases me.

"Put some clothes on. I'm gonna check the room again. See if she left anything." He leaves without another word or even a glance my way, and I slump against the wall to take a few deep breaths.

A tear falls, and dozens follow while I hold back the urge to fall apart entirely in her absence.

Karma has come for me.

It's about fucking time.

Except... it's affecting every single person I care about.

"SHE'S NOWHERE. I've looked within a twenty-mile radius. Asked some friends." Lance sighs and runs a hand through his hair, then slumps against his car door. "Nothing."

"At this point, Miller, I'm inclined to fucking fire you."

"Pierce," River grips my bicep and yanks me to his side. "I swear you're worse than a fucking toddler. Just shut the fuck up."

"I get it," Lance says as his gaze flickers between us. "I do." He raises his hands. "I'd want to knock me out, too. I didn't feel good last night, for a few reasons, and I nodded off when I should have been watching."

"You moth—"

River slaps his hand over my mouth and digs his fingers in extra tight.

I glare at him.

He tightens his hold.

"Jesus..." Phoenix sighs. "Continue, Lance."

"Something was weird. Real fucking weird. So I got in my car, called up my crew. Next thing I know, it's light outside and everyone's yelling down the place." Lance folds his arms over his chest and shakes his head.

I hope he's mad at himself.

If not, I'll be mad enough for him.

"So, what's the next step?" Phoenix, ever the fucking thoughtful one, asks.

"Let me get you guys on a jet back home."

We all turn to look at Mark.

River's surprised enough he lets go of my mouth.

"You have a fucking jet?" I question with a laugh. "Of fucking course you have a jet. What other secrets are you hiding? Huh?"

"Listen here. I understand you're angry, but don't blame me for your problems." Mark pulls Tris into his arms and turns to head back inside. "Let me make a few calls. I can have it ready within an hour."

Phoenix and River shoot daggers at me, but I don't give a fuck.

"I'm over this shit. I'm gonna find my girl and get her the fuck out of dodge."

River grabs me in a hug, and holds so tight that my heart crumbles... and I start to cry.

"Fuck off me," I murmur into his chest, but he only holds tighter.

"It fucking sucks, man," he says. A few seconds pass, and I feel something wet touch my cheek. River sniffles and shakes his head. "We're all fucking scared. If she left of her own accord..."

"That's the only option I'm entertaining right now, River," Phoenix says. "The other is unfathomable, and I'd suggest you keep that thought firmly in your fucking head."

"I'll go in and get the information on this jet," Lance says. His footsteps fade seconds later, leaving me and the guys alone for the first time all morning.

"The fuck do we do?" I whisper.

"Not a goddamn thing we can do, pup," River says. He pulls back and brushes the tears from his eyes with the sleeve of his shirt, then meets my gaze. "We stand strong, find her, then we grovel until we can't grovel anymore."

Phoenix huffs out an irritated sigh. "I told you both we should have ju—"

"And we stop arguing." River grips my shoulder and points at Phoenix. "Whatever the hell happens from here until we have her in our arms again... we're in it together. Period."

"Alright," I mutter as I lean my head against his shoulder for support.

"Got it, Nixy boy?"

"Yeah," he says. "I got it. Now what the fuck do we do? And if Riley's had a jet..."

"The man has clearly wanted to stay hidden, but he knew he needed an out." I shrug when they both look at me. "It's what I would do. I wouldn't fucking sit here for two decades doing nothing and not having a back-up plan. It's fucking Maxwell we're worried about most here, right?" They nod, and I continue. "So, he keeps his resources hidden, never using them. This is his plan Z."

"And he's mad as fuck he has to use it." Phoenix nods his head toward the house and River and I turn to see Mark storming out of it.

A few feet from us, Mark stops and folds his arms over his chest. "Made the call. I'm compromised here, so you boys better have been serious about taking Tris and me with you."

We nod, and his features soften.

"Good. We have half an hour."

"Thought you said we had an hour?" Phoenix asks, raising a brow.

"That was before I got a tip that Maxwell is on his way to this location." Mark turns around and walks back toward the house. "Chop, chop, boys. The time for revenge is drawing closer. The question now is who's getting it?"

"Fucking creepy," River says. He shivers as we follow Mark inside. "You think she was—"

"Don't say it out loud, River," Phoenix growls.

"The other option is that she's done with our sorry asses." River shrugs when we glare at him. "Pick your poison. Either way, it sucks."

"Well," I say as I step into our room, "this all ends with us by her side." I meet River's gaze. "One way or another."

Hey Blue,

Been a while since I wrote you a letter.

Gotta say it's a damn shame.

Truthfully, I don't know why the fuck I'm writing this to you, but it's the only way to get this fucking mass of thoughts out of my head.

River and Phoenix are going just as insane as I am without you here, and we've only been back a few days.

Back at Junk. Back home.

I don't know if you felt at home here or not. Home for me is just where you are and damnit Raven, you aren't here.

I hope you get to read this one day...

Because the alternative isn't sitting well with me.

Later Gator,
Green

# phoenix

"I don't give a fuck what you think, Riley. It's there, installed. You can't fucking fix it." Pierce storms out of the room, flipping everyone off with both hands. "I'm only worried about—"

I raise my hand to stop Mark mid-sentence and sit down on the edge of the small table we put in for him and Tris an hour ago. "It's fine. Let him have his tantrum. I can't promise we'll take the camera out, but I can promise to have Lance lock it down extra tight."

Mark runs a hand through his graying hair and nods. His eyes flick toward his daughter and he blows out a breath. "If Langston sees us here... I can't think about what would happen."

"Only thing I can promise is to keep your daughter safe, Mark. That's it."

He nods solemnly and watches me as I leave.

I don't glance back at the shed once as I tear through the center of our property. Winter is well over and spring has sprung, bringing with it new life.

All the while, we feel the acute absence of Raven and any sanity we may have found over spring break.

A tool clangs against the side of the garage, followed by Pierce's distinct shout of pain and annoyance. He glares at me when I step around the Jeep and raise a brow at him. "Shut the fuck up, Nix," he spits.

"Didn't say anything." As if I have not a care in the world, I lean against the hood and cross my arms.

"What do you want?" He rolls back under the vehicle to tinker with it needlessly, like he's been doing all day.

"You to chill out, for one."

"What else?"

I pull a cigarette from one pocket and a lighter from another. "Raven."

He slides out from under the Jeep and shifts his gaze from me to the cigarette before standing and holding his hand out expectantly. "Give me one of those."

"Could say please," I grumble as I pull another out and light both of them up.

We stand in silence as we fool ourselves into relaxation.

It's been an entire week without Red in our lives, and we haven't found much. In fact, we've discovered very fucking little, and that's the biggest problem.

"Still no sign of Maxwell?" I ask Pierce, though I train my eyes on a scratch on my bike sitting a few feet from me.

He grunts in response, and I turn back to see him shake his head as he exhales.

"Jimmy?" This one needs an answer sooner rather than later.

His hair falls in front of his eyes when he shakes his head again.

"What are we missing, Pierce?"

"No fucking idea, Nix. Not one." He tosses the rest of his cigarette on the concrete and stomps it out before turning and placing his elbows on the hood. Palms covering his face, he lets out a long sigh that I feel all the way through my soul.

"Yeah. Thought so."

River comes out of the loft a second later with a handful of beers. "You guys need to take a break and... Oh. Hey, Lance. What's up?"

Pierce and I straighten our posture as we turn to look at the head of our security team. Sometimes I miss Trip because he just did shit without asking. Or maybe he just only talked to Pierce, and River and I were a bit more clueless.

Lance steps through the open garage door with his hands stuffed into his pockets and a small grin on his face. It disappears the moment I meet his stare, and I only feel slightly guilty. "I was able to get a full read on the school." No one speaks. "Posters are up. We got people looking for her everywhere, but—"

"If your but is about to piss me off, you might want to back up fifty miles," Pierce says. His threats are becoming ridiculous.

"Pup, I swear if you can't act your damn age—"

"I don't care about acting like anything right now. I want Raven back and I'm sick of sitting around here doing absolutely nothing—"

"You re-built the shed for Mark and Tris," River shouts. "You've fixed every vehicle we own, plus some. If you can manage to shut your fucking mouth for two seconds, I'd be even more impressed with your control and how you haven't burned the world down yet."

"We get it," I chime in. "You can't look at both of us and seriously think we don't want to go digging under every rock for her. Hell, we practically did our first day back." I shake my head and rub my temples. Fucking stress headaches. "At the end of the day, Pierce, we're all stressed, but your fucking mouth is the spark on this powder keg, so please—"

"Shut the fuck up," River finishes for me as he slaps a beer in Pierce's hand with a pointed stare.

Whatever arrangement they have going has been helpful, but Pierce is still Pierce and sometimes I wonder if he's learned anything at all.

"Carry on," River says to Lance after another tense silence passes.

"Right," Lance says. He clears his throat and leans against the tool bench on the wall opposite us. "We found out that a few of the Alpha Mu guys are squatting in the frat house. They refuse to leave for anyone, and Starling said it would take a while to get a warrant."

"And a while is time we don't have," I say.

"Exactly. So," Lance draws out as he looks between us, "I think it'd be best if we pull them for chats."

"The fuck is this, *Love Island*?" Pierce rolls his eyes. "We should just bust down the doors and—"

"Get ourselves arrested?" River shakes his head. "Not worth it. If we can't move freely, we can't search for her."

Lance folds his arms over his chest and chews on his lip in thought.

The silence is the worst part about all of this.

"We catch them as they leave," Pierce says.

"I'm listening," Lance replies.

I watch and listen as they hash out a plan to take each guy one by one, interrogate them, and send them packing.

"This serves two purposes," Pierce says as they look over an old blueprint of the house. "One is that we'll be getting the information we need if we find the right person."

"What's the other?" River asks.

"The other is that the house will be empty again and we can comb it for any other clues." Lance nods as he stands back up. "Yeah. This will work. My team will get on it."

"I want on it," Pierce says.

River sits on a stool and tosses his hands in the air. "So you can get hurt?"

Frustration lines Pierce's features as he turns to face River.

Sensing a lovers' quarrel I don't want to be part of, I meet Lance's eyes and gesture toward the loft. It's warm and cozy like Red always likes it. The ache in my chest grows and grows every second she isn't here, and it's without a doubt the hardest trial I've ever been put through.

*Universe, smite me now.*

"What's up?" Lance asks after he follows me into the kitchen.

I work on preparing dinner for everyone, including Mark and Tris. Food is easy, predictable, and brings people together. So I make it hoping to slow the storm, or at least to protect us from most of the damage. If we're all torn apart through this, I don't know if we'll be able to come back. It takes me a few minutes to get everything ready, and Lance stays quiet as I work. Once the meal is in the oven, I turn back to him and grab a towel to dry my hands with. "You find anything about River's parents?"

Lance's face pales as he meets my stare, but he nods and

straightens himself. "Unfortunately, it seems they've gone missing."

"The others? Priscilla, Chloe?"

"Vanished."

"Fuck." I toss the towel down and brace myself on the counter. "It's as if they've all gone into hiding together. How the hell are we missing them, Lance?"

"They have too many resources. Connections out the ass." He runs his fingers through his hair and looks over to the door where Pierce and River's argument finally halts.

Great... the silence means they'll fuck it out and be on the same page for a few hours again.

Lance must have the same thought as me because he fails to hold back a laugh. He covers it with a cough and rests his arms on the counter before looking back at me. "We'll get them all. I sw—"

"Don't swear or promise me a damn thing, Lance. Just get it done. I need my girl back before I burn every building from here back to the west coast."

He nods and moves to stand, halting when I raise my hand for him to stop.

"Dinner will be done in twenty. Bring your crew in. They're exhausted."

"What about—"

"Everyone we're worried about is in hiding, remember?" I turn and grab water from the fridge. "We can take a break."

*Not like an hour will change our world back.*

"HEY, PHOENIX?" Tris asks timidly.

We're cleaning up the dishes while everyone else is in the garage working on the plan for the frat house.

"Hmm?"

She grabs the dish from my hand and rinses it while I start washing another. "Do you think Raven is okay?"

Million dollar question.

"Absolutely," I lie. "She's good at defending herself," for the most part, "and she's resilient as hell." Truth.

"I hope to be her when I'm grown up." Tris giggles as she grabs the last dish. She rinses and dries it, then puts it away as I dry my hands.

"You already are grown up, Tris," I tell her, meeting her eyes so she knows I'm serious. "Your life has just been different. All of our lives have been different. There's no one way to live."

"Your life has been more exciting." She sighs and pulls herself to sit on the counter, then kicks her feet back and forth so her heels thud against the cabinets.

Thud. Thud.

"Not good, exciting," I remind her.

Thud. Thud.

"Still," she says on a sigh, "to have loved and lost like you have…"

Thud. Thud.

"Don't wish something like that on yourself, Tris." I clear my throat and turn to head out of the room before I do something I regret… like demolish the loft so I don't have to hear—

Thud. Thud.

I swear, I'm normally a good guy, but right now…

Thud. Thud.

"Tris! Honey! It's time to head to bed." Mark Riley to my rescue. Again.

She smacks her feet against the cabinets half a dozen more times—probably to annoy me—then jumps down and moves to her father's side, smiling up at me as she passes. "Goodnight, Nixy!" She walks away and shouts goodnights to everyone else.

The door closes behind her, and I press my forehead against the cool wall, breathing out a sigh of relief.

"She gets on your nerves, too, doesn't she?"

Embarrassed does not come close to explaining how I feel when I jump a mile in the air, only to find River standing at the bathroom door.

He laughs and holds his hands up. "Sorry to scare you."

"I'm tired, River. And she does drive me crazy."

"Must be because she's not *her* and it's weird having another woman where ours normally is."

"Why are you so insightful all of a sudden?" I raise a brow at him as I straighten out and start toward the stairs.

Bed. Bed sounds good.

"Someone has to be. And since you've been super grumpy…" He shrugs.

"Goodnight, River," I say as I pass him with a pat on the shoulder.

"Goodnight, grumpykins."

I don't take the bait and head to bed instead.

Sleep is my escape.

# TO: RMHILL@MYEMAIL.COM FROM: UPINFLAMES@MYEMAIL.COM SUBJECT: THE LONGEST WEEK...

Hey. Hi. Salutations.

Red.

Fuck.

I miss you so much. My heart feels like it's bleeding out all over the place.

Nothing feels right without you here, Red. Nothing.

I'm half-tempted to watch the guys fuck just once so I can picture you in the middle, like you often were.

You will be again. I swear on my life.

Which is easy to say because if I'm wrong about you coming back to us... I'd rather be dead, anyway.

I love you,

Flames.

# river

Two weeks.

Two fucking weeks we've been without Rae and I think I'm about to throw everything away in favor of killing the fucker in front of me.

He'd deserve it for being such a spineless asshat.

But Rae wouldn't want me to senselessly murder a dude for following directions.

The real culprit is Maxwell, and we fucking need that cockroach to burn in the depths of hell.

We know he has Rae. There's no other option.

"Where the fuck is she?" I scream into the guy's face as I throw another punch.

He's beaten, bloodied, near-lifeless. He can't talk to me anymore since I'm pretty damn sure he passed out a minute ago when I slammed my boot into his dick.

"River," Phoenix snaps. He grabs my wrist as I thrust it toward the guy again, stopping me right before my knuckles touch the guy's broken nose. "That's enough."

I shake my head and pull my hand from his grip, glaring

at him as I back away. My fingers ache as I run them through my hair.

Again, I don't fucking care.

Life hasn't been easy without her, and my heart aches every time I find Pierce looking off into oblivion like he is now. Like he's given up.

We can't fucking give up.

"Lance is bringing the last guy down now, but I don't think anyone knows where Maxwell is." Phoenix leans against the wall and crosses his arms over his chest. He shakes his head as he studies the newest victim of my fists, then shifts his gaze up to meet mine. "This isn't helping anyone."

"Neither is Pierce's complete silence. No ideas, pup? None at all?" I storm over to him and slap his cheek to get his attention, but he continues staring at the wall like it holds all the answers. When I shift my gaze in that direction, I see nothing but fucking brick.

"River!" Phoenix snaps again.

"Who the hell put you in charge?" I snarl as I spin on him. "Who the fuck said 'Phoenix is gonna be the boss now and we do as he says'? Huh?"

"Someone in this godforsaken crew has to have their head on straight." His voice is monotone, as if none of this is affecting him at all.

I can't fucking handle it.

"Fuck you, Nixy boy. Fuck. You."

He looks about ready to kill me as he stands straight and adjusts his bloodied shirt sleeve. Before he can do anything, the door at the top of the stairs opens and both our gazes land on Lance as he and one of his crew drag another Alpha Mu member down to us.

"Name?" Phoenix asks the second they drop him in the small folding chair.

"Matthew Leatherwood."

I meet Phoenix's gaze, and we both share a knowing grin before looking down at the guy. "One last prank on the Leatherwoods. Send their son home with a broken nose and wet pants." I kick his shin hard enough he shouts inside the black cloth covering his face.

"Why's he here? I didn't even know he was in the frat." Phoenix walks around until he's standing beside me and we're facing the guy down.

"He was posted outside of Jimmy's house." Lance sits on the bottom stair and scrubs a hand through his sweat covered hair. "Joined the frat last month and hasn't left Jimmy's side since."

"Can we get this over with, please?" Pierce asks. He hasn't moved from his spot in the corner, but his glare threatens to kill anyone who puts a pause on his pity party.

"Soon as you get over here and question him," I say, "then sure. C'mon, pup. Show him who he's fucked with."

Phoenix sighs.

"I'm good here," Pierce says instead of manning the fuck up.

"Fucking fine then," I snap. I turn toward Matthew and snatch the bag from his head. "Ooh, that looks like it hurts a bit."

"Fuck you!" His spit lands on my jeans with the rest of his buddies' blood as he glares up at me.

I chuckle and lean forward, pressing my fingers into a spot above his eye that looks particularly painful. That chuckle turns to a full on laugh when he shrinks back from the pain. "I've got my fucking arrangements already, Matty, but I'm flattered. Now," I say as I kneel in front of him, my grip tight on his kneecaps, "tell me where the fuck our girl is."

"That slut hasn't been seen since Jimmy—" he pauses and closes his eyes as if he knows he was about to say something he shouldn't.

"What about Jimmy, Matty boy?" My grip on his knees tightens and he growls at me, even as he whimpers in pain. "Come on. Tell me what the fuck he's done to her."

He shakes his head and tears fall down his cheeks. "I-I-I can't! He'd kill me if I told you anything!"

"We'll kill you for shits and giggles, sunshine." My grin grows wider as I watch his internal struggle, and my grip on his knees grows more painful the longer he battles it out.

"Fuck this," Phoenix says. He picks up a bloodied crowbar from the floor and raises it above his head.

The darkness in him rarely comes out, but when it does, well, should have seen the last guy that crowbar took a liking to.

Or... maybe not.

I wince when Phoenix brings the crowbar down hard at Matthew, then bark out a laugh when he doesn't make contact at all and Matty boy pisses himself.

Phoenix gets right in his face, grips his jaw between two fingers, and snarls at him. "Tell. Us. Where. She. Is."

"She's in an old cabin up in the mountains. Two hours from here. Being held by Maxwell and Jimmy and the Legacies. Please, please, please don't kill me. I have... I have dreams, man. Hopes and dreams and—"

I slam my knee hard into Matty's face and grimace as more blood spreads on my pants. Probably gonna have to burn them now. Not even a minute passes before Pierce bounds up the stairs, knocking Lance and his second down in his wake.

"He's gonna make rash decisions we can't afford for him to make," Lance states as he looks at me.

Everyone knows the drill by now; Phoenix is the level-headed one in charge of all the planning; I'm the guy who beats the fuck out of people, but also the one who is in charge of Pierce; and Pierce is the one who has decided to burn the world down in his haste to get to our girl.

But the last few days, he's been quiet.

And now that he's not sulking?

Everyone's in trouble.

"River," Phoenix says.

"Got it." I nod at the rest of them and make my way up the stairs after Pierce. I have an ache he can work on while we wait for plans to be made.

The frat house is quiet as I amble through the shreds of what's left. Beer bottles and other trash scattered everywhere. Dishes busted. Tables and couches ruined. Squatters laid waste here before we claimed it again. We needed to lure the remaining frat members to us so we could interrogate them, and this seemed to be the best way to do it.

"Pierce?" I call as I make my way up the stairs.

Visions of Raven coming down them in her dress for our Royals ball last year flood my mind. While my chest aches with her absence, it also feels the remnants of her love. Each step I make toward the little room Pierce shoved her into reminds me of our moments together. It fills me with remorse and a fierce determination to get her back and spend the rest of my life apologizing.

"Pup?" My voice echoes down the hallway where his room used to be.

Jimmy took it over and plastered dirty pictures of her and other girls all over before the FBI took them all as evidence. They've done nothing with it, of course. They don't care. The frat got shut down, but that was the extent of what happened, and now our girl is missing. Taken from us when we should have kept her close.

A painful cry sounds from Pierce's old room and I take off running toward it. I shove through the door and immediately my eyes fall on him. "Pierce!"

On his knees in the middle of the floor, Pierce clutches onto something wrapped around his hand with blood dripping down his wrist.

"Oh, pup." I sigh as I sit next to him and wrap my arm around his shaking shoulders.

He says nothing, but opens his hand and shows me the bracelet I got him for Christmas. "I-I'm sorry," he whispers as he lifts his eyes to meet mine. "The strand broke when I punched the wall and—"

"Don't worry about it, babe. I've got more where that came from."

"What?" His brows draw up in confusion, but I don't let him think more about it.

I said I'd keep that secret and take it to my grave.

"Let's get out of here, yeah?"

He nods and allows me to help him to his feet while he continues to look around the room we once violated Raven in. "I hate myself for what I did to her."

"I know."

"I'm not worthy of her," he adds with a scuff of his shoe against the floor.

"Excuse me, what?" My heart hammers in my chest as I

turn to him and lift his chin with my fingers. "What did you just say?"

Forest green eyes glare at me, then dull with sadness as he tries to look back down.

"Tell me what you said, pup. Go on."

"I'm not fucking worthy, okay?" he shouts, tossing his hand out. The bracelet flies across the room and the beads fall off.

Fuck, this would be hilarious if he knew he just threw my jizz across the room.

My lips twitch, but I maintain composure as I glare at him. "You are fucking worthy, Pierce Jackson. Worthy of me and her and everything good coming to us."

He snorts and shakes his head. "Yeah, and what good is coming to us, River? All I fucking see is death and loss and—"

"Shut the fuck up," I snap.

"She's gonna be used by him, if she hasn't already," he continues.

I wrap my hand around his throat. "I said shut the fuck up."

"If Maxwell gets his way, Jimmy has already—"

"I said shut up!" I bellow into Pierce's face while gripping his throat harder, forcing him to stop talking when I take his breath away. "Get on your fucking knees."

He rolls his eyes.

"Do I need to make you?"

He swallows, and his pulse races beneath my fingers.

I shove him down to his knees with my free hand on his head, still holding his throat tight in my fingers. His face changes colors, so I'm forced to release my hold on him. "Breathe," I instruct.

A tear falls down his face as he does.

"Good boy." I tighten my hold again and meet his glare with my own. "You're going to put your mouth to good use now. I fucking hate it when you use it to talk shit."

He nods.

I unbuckle my jeans and push them and my boxers down just enough to free my dick, then grab his hand and place it over my shaft. "Get me hard, then put it in your mouth and keep it there."

Pierce does as he's asked, because he'd rather I take his choices away right now. We've talked at length about me getting him out of his own head, and I'm more than fucking happy to deliver.

My eyes stay on his as he strokes me until I'm hard, and I groan when he finally leans forward and stuffs me as far back in his mouth as he can manage. "Fuck," I breathe, threading my fingers through his soft hair and hold on as he bobs his head a few times. "Stop," I command, and he does. "Look at me."

It takes a few seconds for him to do it, but when his eyes meet mine, he's almost pleading for me to distract him. But I can't.

Not this time.

"Are you gonna listen now that your mouth is full of my dick, pup? Answer me," I growl when he doesn't show signs of answering.

He blinks twice for yes, and I slide my free hand down his cheek. My dick jumps when I see the line of blood that trails after my fingers, but that's not the point.

"You are worthy of more than you think." I grip his hair tighter when he tries to pull away. "You have apologized and proven yourself worthy of her, not only in her eyes but mine and Nix's, too." I grunt when he swallows, and another tear falls down his face. "You are worthy of our love, Pierce."

He digs his nails into my thighs and tries to push off, but I knew he would, so I tighten my hold on his hair and thrust my hips until they meet his face and he's forced to stay put. His glare doesn't scare me. Not anymore.

"You are loved, and we will get her back. I won't tolerate you talking like we never will. Like he's already violated and hurt her. And even if he has," I raise my voice when he tries to pull away again, "we'll deliver his head on a platter to the devil himself if we have to."

The room falls quiet but for his heavy breathing.

"Do you understand, pup?"

He blinks twice.

"Now, suck my dick to apologize for running off and breaking the jizz bracelet I made for you." I freeze, and just when I think he took in the bit of information I didn't mean to expose, he wraps his tongue around the head of my dick and I groan. "Good fucking boy," I praise as he takes me to the back of his throat over and over.

He groans, and I look down to see him touching himself.

Normally, if he was being punished, I wouldn't let him. Considering our circumstances, and the way he listened so well, I let him have his release.

His mouth is warm heaven for me. His saliva coats my dick, and when he swallows, it squeezes in all the right places. When he pulls his own dick out, I watch in fascination as he angrily tugs at it, as if he's mad that he's hard right now.

"Fucking come for me like a good boy," I order as both of our movements speed up and become erratic.

His eyes latch onto mine just as he hollows his cheeks

and sucks me to the far reaches of infinity, and I come down his throat with a barely contained shout.

I watch with heavy-lidded eyes as he comes on himself. "Good boy," I praise him again as I lean down and grab his wrist, licking his cum from his hand. His eyes glaze over for a moment and I lean in to kiss him, grinning when he allows me to thrust my tongue into his mouth and force him to taste himself. When I pull back, he's glaring at me, and I quickly put my dick away.

"What did you mean by a jizz bracelet?" he asks as he adjusts himself.

"Nothing." I turn and rush out of the room with him fast on my heels.

At least he's thoroughly distracted now.

Hey, RaeRae.

I know your phone is literally sitting next to me right now, but fuck, sweet girl.

I fucking miss you.

I've kept Pierce as together as possible, but he looks like he's drowning more and more every single day.

He's not the only one.

Maybe when you get back, we'll all learn how to swim again, yeah?

I guess we have to teach Tris how to do that, too. There's a lot she doesn't know.

Fuck... I miss you.

I love you.

We'll see you soon. I swear it.

# raven

Blinding lights turn on again, and I squeeze my eyes tight in an attempt to keep my eyesight.

Doesn't work.

Never fucking does.

"Good morning, sugar," Jimmy says as he makes his way over to me.

The scent of bacon and eggs calls to my empty stomach, but I ignore it. I've been ignoring it for days now, and even after he hurts me again and again, I refuse to take a damn thing he gives me. It takes my own fucking mother to come down here and force food into my mouth.

Not like I give a shit about her, either.

"We have the best doctor here to see you today, sugar. He swears he can get your voice back! Isn't that exciting?" He sits down on the bed next to me and holds up the plate. "Isn't it exciting, sugar?" There's an edge to his voice now, the same one he gets every morning when I don't respond, in any fashion, to him.

I glare directly into his eyes, the same as I have every morning I've been here.

It's been fourteen days since he stole me right from under everyone's noses.

Thirteen of those I've been in this basement.

Twelve of which have been with me in chains, because I almost murdered Jimmy the second I could.

I grin at that thought, then wince when the devil himself grips my jaw.

"Better be me you're smiling for, Raven." He leans in and kisses me, and I freeze.

Deer in fucking headlights freeze.

I don't move a muscle as he tries to pry his tongue into my mouth.

And fuck does it suck to hold my breath this long, but I don't want to smell his slimy-ass as he assaults me.

Just as he starts to get rough and move his hands further down to places I don't want him, the door at the top of the stairs swings open.

"To be continued, sugar," Jimmy whispers before standing and looking over at Maxwell.

"Good morning, dear children. I have an announcement!" He smiles brightly when he sees food next to my face, as if my hands aren't bound to the bed above me. "Glad to see you're eating, sweetheart."

I'm not, but okay.

I nod once and give him a tight smile. If I play along and don't anger the beast, they'll leave me here and send down the woman who birthed me to feed and bathe me.

Like I'm a fucking animal.

Wish I could snarl like one. Bet they'd think twice before allowing Jimmy to—

"What do you mean, you're letting her go?" Jimmy shouts.

I blink. Must have missed the conversation.

"She's going to move upstairs, and Priscilla is going to work on helping her clean her wounds. She needs to be presentable for the ball in a few days." Maxwell, my slimy-ass father, grins as he wraps his hand around Jimmy's arm. "Let's go upstairs." He meets my eyes, and his smile grows. "You've survived so much these past few months, sweetheart."

*Yeah, thanks to you, asshole.*

"I'm so proud."

I can't help but snort a laugh, and his eyes narrow. I pretend to cough after that, and he nods before turning to move up the stairs with Jimmy. He whispers in Jimmy's ear, and they both look back with evil grins before Jimmy turns back toward me.

Well, this can't be good.

"Dad says that if you play nicely with me, you can come upstairs now instead of later."

What are we, children? I close my eyes and take a deep breath, then give Jimmy the innocent look of 'please help me' he always wants from me.

He perks up while, behind him, Maxwell nods his head and makes his way back up the stairs.

"Oh, the fun I'll have with you, sugar." Jimmy strips his clothes down, and not for the first time, leers over me like I'm his property.

Only this time, just like the last two, I don't fight.

Compliance is the easy way out, but it's easier on my body than last time.

So I let my mind go blank and pretend like everything is

okay as he does what he wants with me. I force the tears to stay back and my heart to hold strong... while my body takes the brunt of his assault.

"C'MON, RAE!" *Pierce shouts for me as he runs out of the backyard fence.*

*"Just a minute!" I yell.*

*"It's not sneaking out if you ask for permission, young lady," my mom says as she leans against the doorframe to the kitchen.*

*"Yeah, I know." I roll my eyes and grin up at her. "I just don't want you or Miss Jackson to worry."*

*"Does he know you tell us?"*

*I shake my head. "Absolutely not. If the worst thing Green ever does is sneak out to go play at a playground, I think he'll survive the teen years!"*

*Mom laughs and ruffles my hair before ducking back inside. "He's looking for you, little bird."*

*"Be back in a bit," I say quietly before turning on my heels and taking off like a bat out of hell to catch up with him.*

*"Little bird," Pierce calls. I love that he took on my mother's nickname for me. She'll forever live on in that name.*

*Not that she's dying anytime soon. I won't let her.*

*I go real still and quiet as I enter the woods surrounding our favorite spot. I don't want him to find me too soon.*

*"Little bird, I know you're here."*

*A twig snaps near me, and I scramble back toward another tree, hoping he didn't hear and will walk right past me.*

*An eternity passes, and I let out a breath, then squeal when my legs go flying in the air as Pierce wraps his arms around me.*

*"Caught you, little bird. Didn't fly far, did you?" He kisses my cheek and laughs when I giggle.*

*I fix my shirt when he places me back down on the ground and cross my arms as I glare at him. "You cheat!"*

*"How can I cheat when you make it so easy to find you?"*

*"Yeah, well," I scoff. "One day, Pierce Jackson, I will make it super hard for you to find me."*

*A serious expression passes over his face, then he looks down at me and grins. "Nah, little bird, I'll always find you."*

"MAXWELL, PLEASE," Priscilla whines as he paces up and down the hallway outside of the room I'm staying in.

I'm just glad it's my own and not with Jimmy.

He said I could have it since I've been playing so well, so I guess some good did come from me allowing that asshole to abuse my body.

"It's all her fault, Priscilla. All of it!"

I flinch at the serious anger in his tone. My fight-or-flight kicks in, but instead of doing either of those, I freeze at the sight of my father walking through the door and glaring at me.

"You told them!" he yells.

I shake my head back and forth repeatedly.

"You fucking told them!"

"How could she have, baby?" Priscilla asks as she lays a hand on his arm.

"Get the fuck off of me!" He rounds on his precious wife and backhands her hard enough to send her to the floor. When he looks over at me, his shoulders slump, and he sighs. "Sweetheart, why would you tell them we've taken you?"

I shake my head again as I back away from him.

"Do we need to put you back in the basement?"

I shake my head.

"Actually, dad," Jimmy chimes in as he enters the room, "it was my fault."

Maxwell's eyes fall to slits before he turns toward Jimmy. "Explain," he commands.

Jimmy swallows hard, looks at me, then squares up to Maxwell. "One of mine, sir. He was posted outside of my mom's house. They... they got to him."

"And what did you do with him?"

"Brought him here so you could punish him," Jimmy says quietly.

"You fucking what?" Maxwell grabs Jimmy's throat and pushes him against the wall. "You realize you led them right to us, right? You gave them our position. One we've held for weeks now."

"I-I'm sorry, sir."

I'm at the point where I'd love to see Jimmy shit his pants right about now, but I keep my composure as the scared little girl and watch with glee as Maxwell gets in his face.

"The ball is in three days, Jimmy. I expect you to be married and giving me an heir before summer. Do you hear me?"

Jimmy nods.

"Good. Now, I'll go take care of this spineless child." He tosses Jimmy to the floor and rights himself. Just before he leaves the room, he looks back at me. "I apologize for thinking you betrayed me, sweetheart. I'll make up for it at dinner tonight." He spares one last glare for Jimmy, then shakes his head and walks out of the room. "Come, Priscilla," he orders, and she scrambles up and rushes after him with her hand on her cheek.

"Your fuckboys have caused me too many problems, sugar," Jimmy says as he walks over to me. He leans in and grins when I shiver. "For every one of my boys they fuck with, I'm going to fuck you." He bites down on my shoulder and I toss my head back. Not in pleasure, but to keep the tears at bay. "For every time I get in trouble with dad, I'm going to punish you."

I inhale a sharp breath and close my eyes against the assault of his hands sliding between my legs.

"You're mine now, sugar. They won't have you again." He pulls back and uses his free hand to grip my face, forcing me to look at him. "Do you understand me?"

I swallow and nod once.

His lips curl into a lazy grin, and he kisses my cheek before letting me go. "Now, go get ready. Dinner is in a few hours, and we have so much to do before our own announcement."

He leaves the room, slamming the door behind him, locking it as he goes.

I slump to the floor and study every inch of the room as I fight back the urge to crumple up and cry.

Boys,

This letter is hard to write. I don't exactly know where I am or if I can even fucking get this to you, but I need to write something.

Anything.

I'm scared. I haven't been this scared since mom got sick...

I hope you're coming soon, because Maxwell sa—

# *pierce*

P eople.

So many goddamn people in my fucking space.

And no one has Raven, so it's pointless.

All of this is pointless.

"Hey, Pierce," Tris says as she sits next to me.

I turn my head and raise a brow at her, waiting for her to speak. It's the most I can do these days.

"Just wondering if you're doing okay..."

"Absolutely."

"Oh? Well, good." She fidgets with her hands in her lap for a few moments, then looks over at me and narrows her eyes. "Sarcasm?"

"Good job figuring that one out all by yourself."

"You're a jerk," she spits before standing and stomping off.

"And you're annoying," I shout at her back.

River sits next to me and wraps his arm around my shoulders. His hot breath rolls across my neck and I shiver. "You're an asshole and I want you to go apologize to her."

I roll my eyes and move to stand, but he holds me down with his hand firmly on my shoulder and the other clasped on my knee. When I glare at him, he only grins. "I'll go apologize."

He shakes his head and tightens his grip. "You'll apologize when you mean it. Anyway, everyone is out in the garage making plans and you're in here sulking."

"I'm not fucking sulking." I fold my arms over my chest for a split second before scoffing and dropping them.

"Come on. Sam has some information to share with the rest of us." He yanks me to a stand and pulls me behind him into our garage.

My fucking sacred space that everyone seems to have taken over.

The bikes are off to the side, the Jeep is out in the yard, and there's a foldout table sitting in the center like it's a conference room, complete with my security team, Starling, and a few FBI guys who have been with us for the last few months.

They've all been put on leave, which worries me, but they seem to be here for a good cause, and that cause is finding Raven and bringing her back to us.

"Nice of you to join us, Jackson," Agent Starling says. He chuckles when I glare at him and gestures to a seat across from him. "We were just discussing if we should put cams on you boys, or just leave it at wires."

"Why can't we just go in there and steal her back?" I snap.

"Well—" Starling starts to say, but I don't want to hear his bullshit.

"Because you're all fucking pussies and can't charge in there because you're worried about your jobs instead of the life of a girl. Got it." I move to stand, but River grips my shoulder hard and I wince as I sit back down.

I've allowed him to do this dominating shit, but only because, at the end of the day, he's keeping me in line. He's got Raven's best interests at heart when clearly I don't.

"Are you finished?" Starling asks with a raised brow and a far too cocky grin.

"Yes," I mutter, relaxing in the chair.

"Good. As I was saying, Sam has the thought that we should put cams on you boys, but Lance—"

"I know," Lance interrupts, "that Maxwell will already be looking for cameras and wires. Putting the brand of wires on that Sam wants will help, as they're virtually unde-tectable at the moment, but—"

"Cameras are Maxwell's specialty," Trip chimes in. He sits back and folds his arms as he grimaces. "Maxwell has stock in too many camera developers to not know what to look for. If you three show up, well," he shrugs.

"Well, what?" I ask through gritted teeth.

"He'll look you over head to toe before allowing you into the building."

"He won't be allowing us to do anything," River says. "We're going to walk right in the doors and, because it's a party, Maxwell won't want to make a scene."

"So you're going to make a scene and hope he doesn't make one back?" Trip raises a brow and rubs the bridge of his nose. "Jesus, I'm so glad I moved on from you idiots."

Starling chuckles and twirls his mustache.

A few minutes pass as we all think it over.

"No cameras," Lance says. "Nothing will hold in court, anyway. Everyone here isn't supposed to be working."

"He's right," a burly man at the end of the table says. His

dark eyes land on me. "We're here because we know what's happening and we don't like it. We can pool our resources, kid, but anything we catch on the wires is only useful for information, not court proceedings."

I glance over at Starling. "Seriously?"

He sighs and places his forearms on the table as he meets my gaze. "All we can do is scare them at this point."

"Then how the fuck do we plan on arresting Maxwell?" I ask, standing and slamming my fists on the table. "What the fuck is the point of all this?" I gesture around at everyone. "Huh?"

"Pierce," River calls in warning.

I spin and glare at him. "Nah. I'm not wasting my fucking time. I'm gonna go get her, take his ass down, and—"

"ENOUGH!" Phoenix shouts as he stands and makes his way toward me. "I've got the plans. You just fucking follow them like a good little *pup*." He hisses the last part and I rush him, only to be held back by River and Lance. Phoenix sighs and looks at the rest of our audience. "I apologize for the interruption."

River pulls me into the loft and up the stairs without a word. He tugs me into the bathroom, puts me in the shower, and turns the cold water on.

"What the actual fuck?" I shout, scrambling to get out.

"Stay the fuck in there and cool off." He glares at me from his position at the shower door. The water splashes onto him, and goosebumps rise up his forearms, but he says nothing and does nothing. Just... glares.

I hate when River's angry.

Hell, I hate when I'm angry.

"Riv—"

"Shut the fuck up."

"River—"

"You know," he says with a soft laugh, "I would like to be part of the shit going on down there. Did you know that?"

I blink in confusion, because he's the one who brought me up here in the first place.

"But I'm up here tending to you. Making sure you don't fucking kill anyone." He glares at me again. "You're a fucking child, Pierce. You're not helping anyone, and instead of me knowing what the hell's going on, I'm depending on Phoenix, who has his shit together by a mere thread but is holding us all up. I'm tired of it."

"River, I'm—"

"You're not fucking sorry!" he shouts in my face. Our noses slam together hard as he gets as close as possible to me. "You're never fucking sorry."

"What the hell is that supposed to—"

"Hell, half the time I wonder if you're actually sorry about assaulting Raven, or just sorry that everyone you fucking care about was pissed off. So you apologized in order to get away. Or that your dick wasn't getting wet enough, so you said sorry to get back—"

"I said I was sorry for that a million and one times, and I'll keep saying it." I drop to my knees and stare up at him, shocked that he'd say such horseshit when he saw what I went through for their acceptance.

"Yeah, well, if you keep acting like a child, Pierce," he sighs and kneels down until our faces are mere centimeters apart. "If you keep acting like a child, I'm going to lock you up the way you did her. Then we'll go save her without you."

My entire body chills, and not from the water, when

River stands and storms out of the bathroom, slamming the door hard in his wake.

Was I hoping he'd use his dick to shut me up again?

Yes.

Was I thinking I'd get off and forget all the things for a few seconds?

Also yes.

I'd never have thought he'd leave me on the floor like this, empty, broken, and alone.

I hated being alone.

"OH, *c'mon, silly. It'll only be a day or two,*" Rae says. She pats me on the head like a dog and saunters over to her friend's car. *"You'll be fine all by yourself."*

Yeah, but you won't.

*"If you say so, little bird."*

*She blushes at the use of her nickname, and I grin. Her friend shouts for her to climb in, and she does so, blowing me a kiss just as they round the corner at the end of the street.*

*My phone buzzes, and I groan, knowing exactly who it is before I even pull the damn thing out of my pocket.*

*Every time someone leaves me alone, it's like this fuck has a sixth sense and uses it against me.*

*"Yeah?"*

*"Watch your tone with me, Jackson,"* the asshole snaps. He *groans a few times, and I roll my eyes, realizing he's called me while fucking someone again.*

*"Couldn't have waited a few more seconds, old man?"* I grin *when he growls.*

*"Out," he commands the person on the other line, then I hear metal on metal as he probably fixes his belt. "Where's my daughter?"*

*I stare out at the street where she left. "Out with a friend."*

*"And why didn't you go?"*

*"Well, Mr. Langston, sir, it's because girls don't like boys at sleepovers. Unless you really want me, you know, sleeping over with her."*

*"I will beat your ass next time I see you, boy."*

*"No thanks," I snark, knowing it'll only make the punishment worse.*

*Last time he left me on mom's doorstep, broken and bloodied. The only reason I made it inside was so Rae didn't see me like that. She didn't know the dark, depraved nature of her father.*

*"Since you're alone," Maxwell starts to say, and I realize my weekend is about to get shittier.*

*He always makes me do the worst shit when I'm alone.*

"I'M SORRY," I whisper in River's ear as I climb into bed beside him.

He shifts and turns to face me with a frown marring his lips and his brows drawn together. "I'm sorry, too."

"We're falling apart without her."

He nods and pulls me into him. "Yeah, but we won't break. We're just bickering like an old married couple right now."

I snort a laugh. "Imagine being old *and* married."

We fall quiet for a few minutes.

"River?" I ask.

"I have thought about it, pup." His hand snakes around my back and rubs circles over it, easing as much tension as possible. "I've thought about it a lot."

"Yeah," I whisper, smiling when I feel his lips on the top of my head, "me too."

# raven

"I think you're going to like it up here, sweetheart." Maxwell grins as he leans down toward me where I'm sitting at the breakfast table. He snaps his fingers and one of his men hands over a box.

It opens to reveal a beautiful black choker necklace with a sunflower charm dangling in the center.

I flinch back when he moves closer to me, but it doesn't matter to him.

With surprisingly careful fingers, he drapes it around my neck and closes the clasp before standing straight and looking down at me, almost as if he's proud.

I snort. As if.

"Now, sweetheart," he croons as he grabs something else from the box. He shoos his man away and shows me a remote in his hand.

What the fuck?

"Darling," Priscilla calls to him from her place across the table. "This isn't necessary. I'm sure she'll be good." Her eyes land on mine and narrow, as if she's trying to command me.

Tough luck, bitch. You were never my mother.

"Priscilla, I suggest you shut your mouth." Maxwell looks down at me and waves the remote in front of my face. "This should keep you good and obedient, I think. Act out, and I press this button here." He moves his finger toward it and I tense up. "It'll send a little bit of a shock to you."

I glare up at him, only to get a shock sent directly to me, forcing me to wince and curl in on myself. Tears flow down my cheeks and I claw at the necklace, wanting it off. Now.

Sick fuck.

"Be good, sweetheart." He turns to look at my side. "Jimmy?"

"Yeah, dad?" He places his hand on my thigh as he leans toward him, looking up expectantly.

"Keep her in your sights at all times tomorrow. Do you understand me?"

Jimmy nods and tightens his hold on my thigh. "Yes, sir." He looks over at me and his nasty grin grows. "Get that, sugar? You gotta stay in my sights at all times." He leans toward me and brushes his lips against mine, forcing me back into the chair.

When I refuse to kiss him back, he grunts and squeezes my thigh tighter as he leans back in his chair and works on his food again.

The rest of breakfast is uneventful. Glares from my biological mother. Leers from my father and brother. Side-eyes from the staff, as if they're sizing me up, trying to find out if I'm as terrible as the rest of them.

Where the fuck are my boys?

I let out a sigh as I finish the last bite of my toast, then look out of the cabin window at the trees which hide us from view.

"What did the doctors say yesterday?" my father asks with a mouth full of food.

Disgusting pig.

"Oh," Jimmy says, sitting straighter as if he's excited.

I'm fucking not. I heard what the doctors were saying, even if they were directing all of their comments toward Jimmy.

"Because her brain fucked up over something emotional," *nice way of putting it there, Jimmy,* "she has to go through something just as emotional to flip the switch back in her head." He turns toward me and grins as he reaches out and swipes his hand down my cheek. "With our plans tomorrow, I hope it works." Turning back to our father, they share a sly smile, and my stomach churns.

If no one's going to save me, I need a way to save my fucking self.

THE NIGHTMARES CONTINUE, and not only in my head, as I'm primped ahead of tomorrow's party.

I don't know what the hell my father and Jimmy have planned, but with the way they keep grinning, I know I won't fucking like it.

"Your hair is so very pretty, Miss Langston," the young girl brushing through it says.

Yeah. They don't call me Miss Hill here. I've taken on my father's name like a *proper daughter* should. It's horrible and I hate it.

I nod and give her a tight-lipped smile in return.

They know I can't speak, and sometimes that makes people nervous, so they fill the silence with their own awkward comments and I learn way, way more than I probably should.

"You're going to be a beautiful bride for him," she murmurs quietly.

I fight the urge to vomit, and very quickly I realize what they have planned.

"He bought you a beautiful ring. Did you know that?" She continues brushing my hair as she exposes secret after secret. She sighs almost dreamily as she grabs the rollers and begins wrapping my hair up in them. "He must love you very much." Her hand falls to her stomach, and a tear falls before she shakes her head and smiles bright—too bright— in the mirror.

If she's this in love with Jimmy, she can fucking have him.

Too bad I'll be murdering him alongside my men before he ever gets a chance to live a normal fucking life.

I meet my hard stare in the mirror while the girl continues to put my hair up in curlers, murmuring about Jimmy and how amazing he is.

That fucker took too much from me already, and he continues to take.

"OH, SUGAR," *Jimmy says as he slides me out of the car.*
*The bag is still wrapped over my head.*

*I can hardly breathe, and my inability to scream makes this that much worse.*

*"Get her inside the jet, Jimmy."*

*I jerk in his hold. Kick. Scratch. Whatever I can do to get away.*

*"She's been fighting me the whole trip, dad." Jimmy grunts when I smash my elbow into his stomach.*

*Maxwell chuckles. "She's got a strong spirit. You'll never get bored, that's for sure." His hand lands on the side of my face over the bag. I can feel his breath as he leans in. "Be a good girl, sweetheart. You'll get what you deserve."*

*I wish I could growl at him, but since I can't, I bring my leg up and kick him as hard as I can.*

*He grunts, then laughs and pats my cheek. "Put her in the basement," he tells Jimmy.*

*"But darling," a woman says.*

*"But nothing, Priscilla. Shut your mouth and go back inside."*

*"Hear that, sugar?" Jimmy whispers in my ear. "I'll get to tie you up again, like I've been dreaming."*

I SHIVER JUST THINKING of the night they brought me here, but then my lips quirk up into a devilish smirk.

Whether my men show up or not...

Revenge will be mine.

# phoenix

I stare across the table at our security team, whatever half-assed FBI agents we've made friends with, and Starling and his guys sit on another end. Then there's River, Pierce, and me sitting on the end with our backs to the wall, looking at the guys like we're dreaming.

It amazes me we're even worthy of this much effort, but karma is swinging our way.

Finally.

As if they know I'm thinking this way, both River and Pierce look over to me and show off almost identical half-grins.

I'm happy they've stopped bickering, but it's mostly because we have a massive crew helping us get our girl back. By doing so, the FBI agents involved could lose their jobs in the process. But they're still here. Still tossing their own time and resources out here to find her, because they know all the horrible shit Maxwell Langston has gotten up to over the years, and someone is about to take him down every single inch of his high horse.

"I need you boys to give us at least thirty minutes from the time you walk in till the time you grab her and walk out." Starling pins us three with a look, but he stares at Pierce the longest. At this point, we're all at risk of bursting in there and grabbing her without a second thought.

"I'll give you ten," Pierce retorts, not even giving the man the courtesy of meeting his eyes. He continues to pour over the blueprint of Maxwell's cabin, brows pinched together in frustration or concentration. Could be either at this point.

"Jackson," Trip says as he stands.

Pierce's eyes lift to meet his.

"I brought Starling in to help you, but if you won't listen to him—"

"You brought strangers in and *left*, Trip," Pierce snaps. "You left, and we both know you could have prevented this bullshit."

"Listen," Trip snarls, leaning over the table. "I don't have to listen to your toddler tantrums anymore. I had a sick as fuck kid, and I took her the hell away from here so she could have the best fucking doctors money could buy."

"It was my fucking money you bought it with!" Pierce roars, shoving to his feet and leaning over the table to glare at Trip.

"It was Maxwell's money and you know it." Trip sighs and sits down, rubbing the bridge of his nose. "I was in with him. I was in with you. But the one place I wasn't *in* was my fucking daughter's. So yeah, I ditched you, but I found you the best fucking men I could." He looks up at Pierce, and the exhaustion shining in his eyes stuns me. "I was with you for a long time, Jackson, but it almost cost me my daughter. So forgive me for not catering to your shit for the last few months." He stands again, taps the table next to Starling, then walks out of the room with his head hung low between his shoulders.

Awkward silence takes over the room.

"Well," Starling says. He clears his throat and looks over at Pierce, who finally sits down with a huff. "I'd like to give these guys time to surround the house. Once you guys step inside those doors, Maxwell will have all of you watched closer."

"Which will distract enough of them so we can take out the remaining few," Lance chimes in. His stare is firmly on Pierce. Calculating. Dissecting what just happened.

Probably feeling like shit because Pierce hasn't ever appreciated Lance as much as he did Trip.

Pierce just nods, not saying anything else for the rest of the meeting as we come up with a Plan A, B, and C.

But the guys and I are on the same wavelength; it's all about getting her out as soon as possible.

Fuck protocol. We're getting our girl back.

"YOU THINK she'll be mad at us for taking so long to get her?" River asks.

We're sitting around the kitchen island, stuffing our faces because we might not have time to eat again until tomorrow.

It's a two-hour drive to the mountains, and the party starts in three.

Three hours until we can have our girl in our arms.

Fuck, it's been a long two weeks.

"She'll be livid," Pierce replies. A grin plays across his

lips, and he snorts a laugh before taking a sip of his coffee. "But she'll be happy, too."

River sighs and places his forearms on the countertop, smiling like a dope as if we aren't about to prepare for battle.

"Let's go get our shit on," I tell them both as I finish the last bite of my sandwich. It sits heavily in my stomach alongside my nerves.

Right before I put my foot on the stairs, I catch Starling, Trip, and Lance huddled together inside the garage having a serious conversation. No raised voices, but plenty of angry faces. Especially after Trip shakes his head again and again and shoves Starling's hand off of his shoulder.

*Interesting.*

Lance turns my way and exits the tense conversation, then walks inside and leans against the wall next to me.

I lean against the railing and cross my arms, raising a brow as I wait for him to speak.

"Trip got word about Xavier Hayes," he says, a hint of caution in his tone.

"And?"

"There's genuinely nothing we can do. Apparently, Sommers and Langston had something over the guy. Until we figure out what that is, we can't make a move."

I nod a few times and lick my lips as I think. Surely once we take them both down, their evidence won't stand. "We need a damn good lawyer for him."

Lance nods, then looks down at his phone when it buzzes in his hand. His brows pinch together, and he sighs before stuffing it in his pocket.

"Everything okay?"

He nods once. "Yeah. Tris is just mad that I'm leaving and not taking her with me."

I snort a laugh and pat his shoulder. "Welcome to the world of a woman having your balls, man." One step up the staircase and I turn back to him with a wicked grin. "On your knees at a woman's feet is the greatest place to be."

His cheeks burn bright as he clears his throat and turns away.

I make my way up the stairs with a shit-eating grin contrasting the sour mood I've been in since the night before they took Red from us. I put on the attire for this party, which just so happens to be the same tuxedo I wore to the speakeasy in Vegas. Only this time, there's a bullet-proof vest, and a wire attached to me.

Starling and Trip had wires threaded through our lapels, and they'll attach to a metal pin to hide everything. Nothing too flashy, but a statement piece that will remind Maxwell and Jimmy of who the fuck Raven belongs to.

*Spoiler alert: it isn't them.*

Once I've got my hair up in a half bun, pieces hanging at my sides and down my neck, I meet my eyes in the mirror and take a deep breath.

*Hold on, Red. We're coming.*

# raven

My hands are shaking.

My stomach is churning.

My head is spinning.

I don't know what all these assholes have planned. I'm allowing this girl to slather makeup on my face, spray hairspray until I'm choking, and help me into a black floor-length gown that hugs my body so tight I can't breathe.

She's treating me as her own life-sized Barbie doll, and I fucking hate it. Her eyes are lit up and her grin is big, as if she's having the time of her life doing whatever the Langstons tell her to do. All while fangirling over Jimmy and telling me how lucky I am.

I have a feeling whatever she thinks I'm lucky for... it's not going to sit well with me.

My fingers trace the choker that Maxwell placed over my neck, and I sigh as I think about how he's been using it to train me to do his own fucking bidding.

Stop here, sweetheart.

Take a walk with Jimmy after lunch, Raven.

His attempt to groom me into the perfect woman is sick, and I hate it.

Almost as much as I hate Jimmy for crawling into bed with me so he can use my body every night.

For his pleasure, not mine.

Not that I'd ever get off with him anyway, but he hasn't even tried.

Wham. Bam.

There were no 'thank you, ma'am's.

My eyes bore into the top of the girl's skull as she bends to help me into a pair of black heels. She ties the straps on my ankles, then stands and brushes her hand down the dress to flatten any creases.

I have to appear perfect, after all.

"I'm so excited for you," she breathes again. This time, a hint of sadness bleeds out, and a tear falls down her face that she's quick to brush away. Her hand falls to her stomach again as she turns and gestures out of the door. "After you, Miss Langston."

I roll my eyes at the name and walk out of the door, only to bump into Priscilla.

She looks me up and down, appraising, taking stock, ensuring I don't sully her name more than I already have, then nods once and walks down the hall. No doubt expecting me to follow her.

I have to play my part, so unfortunately I do exactly as she expects. Following her down the hall and toward Maxwell's study, I note more guards, their faces neutral as they allow a sick man to take ownership of people the way he does.

People will do almost anything for money.

"Hello, wife," Maxwell says as we enter the room. "Ah, sweetheart, you look wonderful!"

He's not talking to his wife anymore.

My skin aches to be burned from my body as he wraps me in his arms and collars my throat, ensuring his torture device is firmly in place. When he pulls back, he gives me a once over, then releases me and turns back toward his desk.

"Jimmy should be here in a moment, but in the meantime, dear daughter, I'd like to remind you to be on your best behavior." Maxwell's grin as he turns around makes my stomach drop to the floor, and I sigh as I watch him pull the remote from his pocket and wave it around.

"Is that really necessary?" Priscilla asks, as if she's exhausted by him.

He glares at her and presses a button, sending me to my knees with the force of the shock to my neck.

I pant, claw at it, and fight back tears, because I don't want to ruin the makeup and anger him more. After a few seconds, I glance up at him through my lashes and simply glare. I glare with the heat of a thousand suns and with every death scenario I can think of mixed together.

He chuckles as he leans down, gripping my jaw. "Dear daughter, you shouldn't stare at me that way. Now, stand on your feet and wait for Jimmy to collect you in the hall. I have to deal with," he shifts his gaze to the side, "your mother."

I scramble to my feet and rush out of the room, wincing when I hear a loud *smack* from inside the room. I tune the rest of their argument out as I work to calm my breathing and remember that he placed the remote back in his right pocket.

Never once have I pick-pocketed someone, but I could start today, I'm sure of it.

He has the key attached to the remote on the back, since he and Jimmy pass the thing around like it's a game controller. So once I have it, I can free myself.

It's just grabbing it that will be hard.

Especially with all the eyes on us tonight.

"Hey there, sugar," Jimmy croons as he walks down the hall. He's wearing a tuxedo much like the ones the boys wore in Vegas a few weeks ago.

My heart squeezes in my chest and I close my eyes, fighting the urge to cry.

"You look beautiful," he says in my ear, slinking his hand up to my jaw. Leaning back, he grins and kisses me once, twice, three times before pulling away and knocking on the door to Maxwell's office.

They share a look as Maxwell hands Jimmy the remote to the shock collar, then Maxwell is back in his office and Jimmy is escorting me toward the grand staircase.

So many people are here, I wouldn't be able to breathe on a normal occasion. As it is, I'm on the arm of a complete asshole who has a plan I've yet to figure out.

We make our way down the stairs, and I play the part, because not a single person here is going to save me. They're all here for a party, an announcement, and to show off the other girls on the arms of politicians and influential figures who aren't there of their own volition.

I've quickly learned that Maxwell deals in drugs, guns, and people.

Particularly young women who get brought in from the frat.

It's disgusting, and I hope I get the chance to stab him in the dick before either of us dies.

"Jimmy," an older man calls. I recognize him as the man escorting Lexi down the hospital hallway all those months ago. He wears a three-piece suit and a strong scowl, as if he doesn't want to be here.

"Mr. Sommers," Jimmy greets him politely, shaking his hand. He stuffs his hand inside of his pocket and I dart my eyes down to catch the movement of his fingers as he messes with the remote.

I need to get that damn thing.

"I haven't seen your father around," the older man says. His eyes rake over me, then meet Jimmy's gaze with a raised brow.

Jimmy shrugs while his lips curl into a grin. "He's dealing with his wife." His hand tightens on my waist at the word *wife*, and I get a sinking feeling in my gut.

"Speaking of wives," Mr. Sommers grumbles as he turns his attention toward a group of older women smiling and chatting together to the side of the room.

Pure decadence oozes in this room, while thieves and sick motherfuckers fill it. Fairy lights seem to float in the air as they criss-cross each other, and a large chandelier lights the entire space. The log cabin vibes are real, and while it would seem cozy to anyone else, it suffocates me.

Jimmy says a goodbye to Mr. Sommers and walks us toward a bar. He orders a beer for himself and a flute of champagne for me. "You can only have one glass," he says. "I need you in the here and now with me, sugar."

I sip at the champagne and glare at his stupid face.

"Ah, ah, ah. Don't make me press this button, sugar." He leans down into my space, pressing his lips against my ear.

"Hurting you makes me hard, but I don't need us to be like that in front of an audience." He backs away and laughs as if he's said something *hilarious* and wraps his arm around my waist again, pulling me back into the growing crowd.

Maxwell comes down the stairs a few moments later with Priscilla on his arm, and another woman greets him at the bottom. She wraps her arms around him in an intimate hug, and he places a not-so-subtle kiss on her neck.

When she turns around, dizziness takes over me and I lean into Jimmy, which he takes as me finally showing him affection. It's not, not even close, but the woman standing next to Maxwell and Priscilla is none other than Pierce's fucking mother.

Chloe Jackson.

She's been MIA for so long, I nearly forgot she even existed. Her house has been abandoned for months now, and after Pierce cleaned it, he locked it up tight so no one without a key could get in.

Her blue eyes are striking against her pale skin, and her black hair hangs over her exposed shoulders. The dress she wears pushes her chest up and hugs her backside, much like the dress Priscilla is wearing. Like the one Maxwell forced me into.

How many people does this asshole control?

I'm lost in my thoughts, so when Jimmy calls my name and tightens his hand on my waist, I jump and he chuckles, but glares at me.

"I'm sure you remember Miss Jackson, sugar?" he asks, nodding in her direction.

I nod and hold my free hand out to her, but she pulls me in for a hug instead. My back stiffens and I leave my hands at my sides.

This woman helped destroy the boy I once knew, and while things were finally changing for the better, he'll never be even close to the same. I should stab her with one of the heels I'm wearing.

"I'm so sorry you're caught up in this, sweetheart," she whispers in my ear before pulling back. The regret and sadness in her eyes pisses me off, and I fight to keep from rolling mine.

"Well," Maxwell says with a soft chuckle, "I'd say it's about time to have our announcement now that everyone's here. Don't you, Jimmy?"

Jimmy grins and tightens his hold on my waist as he spins us around and walks us toward the center of the room.

A band is playing a soft song, and some couples are dancing.

He forces my arms around his neck and pulls me in close, his breath fanning over my cheek as he rotates us in an awkward middle-school sway.

I close my eyes and rest my head on his chest, much like I did when we were at our junior prom. Except this time, it's not consensual, and I'm not using him to piss off my best friend. I'm here without a clear plan of escape, surrounded by disgusting and ruthless motherfuckers who most likely won't think twice before ratting out my escape.

So I stay put.

Jimmy slides his hands down my back, toward my ass, and I grit my teeth. He kisses the top of my head and grinds against me, rubbing his hard dick against my front as if he has permission to do so.

I guess here... he does.

While he's distracted, I slide my hands down his sides, hugging him close, showing him the affection he's clearly starved for. It spurs his own touching on, but I don't care. I need to get the fucking remote.

"I knew you'd come around, sugar," he croons in my ear as he pushes further into me.

I glance up at him and our gazes meet just as I stuff my hand in his pocket and grab the remote with one hand while squeezing his dick as hard as I can with the other. I grin wickedly when he winces at the pain, then I go a step further and twist, bringing the motherfucker to his knees.

Not wasting this chance, I spin and rush toward the bathrooms, keeping my eyes down. I don't need to see sympathy or worry or anger. I just need to escape.

Once I'm halfway down the hall, I push into a room and exhale deeply when I find it empty.

Unfortunately, just as I'm about to slam it closed, Jimmy pushes in behind me and spins me, slamming me into the wood and grabbing the remote from my hand. He presses the button, shocking me until my knees buckle. He holds me up with a hand on my waist and one around my throat as he leans into me. "You can't escape me that easily, sugar. We're in it for the long haul, *wife*."

I attempt to recoil, my head smashing against the wood and sending sparks into my vision.

"Oh, you didn't catch on yet? Yeah," he says, grinning. "I'm going to march you back out there, get on my knee for you, and you're going to agree to marry me. It's going to be just us for the rest of our lives, sugar."

Tears spring free as I shake my head. I'd rather die, but I can't tell him that because I can't fucking talk and this is the first time since he kidnapped me two weeks ago in which that fact has truly devastated me.

I was getting to a new normal with the guys, but it's all destroyed.

All of it.

"They're expecting us," Jimmy says. He pulls away and fixes his own clothes, then mine, ensuring he slides his knuckles over my breasts and slightly between my legs. He stands to his full height again and narrows his eyes at me. "I'm going to get on my knee only once for you, sugar, then we're going to find a nice, quiet space, and you're going to get down on yours for me. It'll be your new favorite position, sugar."

I'm defeated.

Truly.

I nod once, giving into the numb feeling encroaching on all of my senses as I take his arm and allow him to escort me back into the main room where Maxwell stands, glaring in our direction.

His face lights up and he lifts a champagne flute, hitting it with a fork a few times so the *tink, tink, tink* sound rattles in my bones.

"I have a quick announcement to make before we begin the celebrations tonight," Maxwell speaks loud enough so everyone can hear him. "You may ask what we're celebrating, and well, you'll find out soon. I want to thank you all for being here tonight, and for doing business with me for all these years. It's almost time to pass the torch, so to speak. My wife has been begging me to take her on a vacation, and with all that's happened in the last year, well, I think she deserves it." He wraps his arm around Priscilla's waist, pulls her into him, and kisses the top of her head.

She smiles and looks around at the crowd, but her eyes are vacant.

No. Shit. Stop feeling bad for her, Raven. Most of these women made their fucking choices a long time ago.

"I'd like to give the floor over to Jimmy Perkins, my half-son, as he has something he'd like to say." Maxwell hands the microphone over to Jimmy, then backs up a few steps and grins.

"Hello there," Jimmy says into the microphone. He pulls me to his side, much like Maxwell has done to Priscilla. "What I'm about to do has been a long time coming. I met Raven when we were in elementary school, and I knew from moment one that she was who I was meant to be with." The crowd *swoons* and his grin grows. "While we share a father, and some look down on that, I only think it's what made us grow closer over the years. She was my date to junior prom. We lost our virginity to each other."

*Doubt that.*

"Everything that has happened has been kismet, really. I fell in love with her and stayed in love with her, and I'm only grateful she's found her way back to me recently."

Releasing me, Jimmy falls down to one knee, grabbing a ring box from his pocket and pulling it out. He opens the box and shows off the largest square diamond I've ever seen, and I contemplate puking in his face.

It'd serve him right for that stupid speech and all the lies, not to mention this ring does *not* fit my personality at all.

I don't even attempt to fake surprise, or a smile, or anything other than disdain for this man.

He glares at me, but quickly fixes his face with an adoring grin. "Raven Marie Langston," he breathes into the microphone, sending shivers up my spine, and not the good kind. "Would you please make me the happiest man on earth by becoming my—"

*BANG!*

The front doors swing open and reveal the three men my soul sings for, and the happy tears meant for a real proposal spring free while behind me, the room descends into shocked silence.

## river



"Just put the goddamn thing in your ear and let's go!" I shout at Pierce as we continue our quick walk toward the cabin.

We may or may not have taken off through the woods after making excuses that we needed to use the bathroom.

Starling's a smart guy, so I'm disappointed in him for even believing that bullshit.

"It's irritating as shit," Pierce grumbles as he stuffs the earpiece back in, shaking his head to check that it's there to stay.

"You know what's annoying as shit?" Phoenix asks. He doesn't wait for us to answer before continuing. "You. Both of you. Stop fucking bickering."

"By bitching right now, Nixy boy, you're doing the exact thing you're telling us not to do." I grin when he turns his head to glare at me.

Rolling his eyes, he turns back and straightens as the cabin comes into view.

Nerves roll around in my stomach and I have this distinct feeling that I should turn around and make new plans. There's no doubt in my mind that my father is inside, dragging my drugged up mother with him and parading around with a proud grin on his face.

I shiver, then straighten up and harden my resolve to do the exact thing Starling kept telling us not to do; get in, get our girl, get out.

Nothing more. Nothing less.

We will not leave without her, and we aren't about sticking around to hang out with these assholes.

"Are you fucking serious, Jackson?" Starling's voice comes loud and clear in our earpieces.

I look over at Pierce, and he's wearing this cocky smirk I just know is his default setting.

"I'm dead serious," he says to Starling as we continue our trek toward the front door of the cabin.

Fifteen feet until we're in the same building as our girl.

"You're going to get yourselves killed, or worse, your girl!" Starling shouts.

Ten feet.

"No," Pierce retorts. "We're going to get our girl out of there. You can deal with the rest."

Five feet. Phoenix shoots a warning glare to Pierce, then nods toward the front steps where a few guards stand in front of the doors.

Pierce nods. "Listen, Starling. We're about to walk inside. So get your guys here or don't. We're not wasting another second on your plans."

Starling shouts obscenities through the line, calling for his men to speed up their movements and get ready to get in position.

Two feet. A guard looks us over with a furrowed brow, but Phoenix shows them the invite we intercepted from a rather unsuspecting Alpha Mu member.

He wasn't happy to give it up, but when we said we'd consider letting him in the frat if he gave it up, he happily obliged.

Sucks for him. That frat will never get reinstated so long as any of us are alive.

"Ready?" Phoenix asks as we reach the front door.

I look to Pierce.

He nods.

I glance at Phoenix.

He swallows, hardens his gaze, then nods.

Shifting my gaze back to the door, I push it open with force, drawing all eyes to us.

Even those of our girl. She's standing in front of Jimmy, who's down on one knee with a giant rock held out to her.

Assessing the tears in our girl's eyes, and the way her entire body trembles in front of him, I know she doesn't want this. Not at all.

I smile at her. Just for a second, to show her we're really here for her and we'll get her out of this. Then, because the other two are seething with rage, I open my arms and grin as I speak loud enough for my voice to carry through the large room. "Sorry we're late. Our invite must have gotten lost in the mail. Shame the state of the postal office these days."

Maxwell Langston, Head Dick in Charge, steps forward with a tight grin. He looks between Jimmy and Raven, grabs a microphone and addresses the crowd. "Well, I think the two lovebirds need a minute. Don't you?"

The crowd murmurs and a few chuckle as they get back

to their boring conversations, all the while side-eying us as we move toward Langston.

Jimmy takes our girl by the arm and shuffles her to another room, but with Maxwell in front of us and a few guards surrounding us, we can't get her. Not yet.

*Soon,* I sign to her when she looks back at us.

She nods before Jimmy shuffles her around a corner.

Looking back at Langston, I fold my arms and watch as Pierce takes a step in front of Phoenix and me.

"Jackson," Maxwell says.

"I want my girl, asshole," Pierce tells him. He doesn't keep his voice low, and people turn to watch.

"We'll have to have this conversation in another room. My men—"

"Fuck that!" Pierce roars in his face.

"You're making a scene," Maxwell says with a sigh. He raises his hand at someone behind us, and before any of us can turn, we're presented with beers. "Have a drink. Stay a while. But just so we're clear," he turns toward us with a sadistic grin lighting up his face, "she's not leaving with you."

"We'll fucking see about that," Pierce snarks. He grabs the beer and pours it over Maxwell's shoes.

"Still throwing tantrums, I see." Maxwell turns and walks out of the room, encouraging the room to enjoy the cocktail hour.

"Where'd she go?" Phoenix questions, on high alert.

"Jimmy took her around the corner, through that hall." I point in the direction they went, and the three of us take off.

"Stand. The. Fuck. Down." Starling shouts in our ears.

"Not a chance, old man," Pierce snaps back, grinning when we pass through a group of people.

"You're going to ruin the entire plan, and he'll just go free." Starling sighs and gives a few more orders. "I'm begging you to listen."

"I don't want to..." Pierce trails off, stopping in his tracks as his eyes latch onto something. "Mom?"

Phoenix's wide eyes meet mine and we slowly turn to look in the direction Pierce is walking in.

I haven't met his mother. She was MIA before Pierce came to the frat. Well, that's what he told me, anyway. But now, here she stands in a tight black dress with her makeup done up and a bright smile on her face.

And glazed eyes.

I know the state of those glazed eyes. They remind me of my mother's.

"What the hell are you doing here? Where have you been?" Pierce tosses question after question at her, while her face drops and she drinks heavily from the glass in her hand.

"Ah, you've found Chloe," Maxwell chimes in as he walks back into the room. He wraps his arm around Chloe's waist and tugs her tight into his side.

Her eyes drop to the floor for a second before lifting to Pierce. A smile grows on her lips. "I've been with Maxwell, PJ." She places her hand over Maxwell's chest and smiles up at him. "We fell in love a long time ago. Spending time with him like this has been long overdue."

Pierce scoffs and shakes his head, folding his arms as he scowls at his mother. "Glad you forgot about me in the process. Anyone who could fall in love with this asshole is trash in my eyes."

"Watch your mouth, son," Langston spits, face going red.

"I'm not, and never will be, your son," Pierce snarls.

Someone announces dinner is ready, and the crowd turns to head that way.

"It seems it's time to announce the engagement," Maxwell says. He adjusts his suit jacket, then escorts Chloe down the hall. He turns only his face as they continue walking. "Stay if you want, boys. Just know you won't be taking her from me again." With that, he continues into the crowd.

"Let's go get Raven," Pierce snaps, turning on his heel and walking down the hall.

"Pierce," Starling snaps in our ears once more.

Pierce sighs. "What?"

"We can have this asshole behind bars within an hour. Do you really, truly, want to fuck that up?"

Pierce's eyes flash to mine, then Phoenix's, before landing on the hall where our girl was last seen. He shakes his head. "No."

"Stand the fuck down. Give us some time."

"If she gets hurt—"

"It's on me," Starling says.

"Guess we're gonna go have dinner with the scum of the earth." I gesture down the hall, in the opposite direction of Raven and Jimmy.

"Fucking great." Pierce shoves his hands in his suit pants and walks ahead of Phoenix and I.

"River?"

My heart stops.

My gut sinks.

I reach out and grab Pierce's shoulder to steady myself.

"Son?"

I force myself to get lost in the forest in Pierce's eyes. I want to stay there. Forget that voice.

But he'll never let me forget it.

Pierce reaches out, grips my hand, and squeezes once before letting go and nodding once. He's telling me to be strong.

"Hello, father," I say as I turn around, adjusting my suit jacket and straightening my shoulders. I may push my shoulders out a bit. I'm posturing, like he taught me to do in the face of danger.

"What are you doing here?" His gray eyes home in on me, narrowing, narrowing, narrowing. His brow furrows as he concentrates, picking everything apart. Like he always does. "You have a piece of hair on your shoulder. Get that off."

My mother, as usual, says nothing. Her eyes are more vacant than Chloe's, and she quickly looks back down at the floor when my father grips her side, a silent order to stay out of this shit. It's her usual mode; obey the abuser to avoid his hands on you, too.

I still struggle between sympathy and hate for the woman.

Meeting my father's gaze with a hard stare, I reach up with my middle finger and flick the piece of hair off of my shoulder.

He growls low in his throat, then clears it when a group walks by us. He grins in their direction and nods once when they ask if he's coming to dinner. "Best we get the dinner out of the way, son. We have a lot to talk about afterward."

I bark out a loud laugh and shake my head. "If you think I'm going to have a single conversation with you ever again, you're delusional. I'm here for my girlfriend, and I plan to leave the second she's in our arms."

His head cocks back. "Our?" Licking his lips, he looks between the two men standing behind me. Disgust overtakes his features, and he shakes his head. "God wouldn't approve of this, River."

"God wouldn't approve of you either, asshole," Pierce snarls. He reaches out and pulls me back by the shoulder. "C'mon. We have a dinner to suffer through."

"You're extremely rude, young man," my father says, but we aren't listening.

Pierce grabs my hand, twines our fingers together, and holds them in the air as he marches us down toward the dining hall.

When I glance up at our hands, he has his middle finger raised, and I crack a genuine smile before leaning my head against his shoulder.

"How much longer?" Phoenix asks with his fingers pressed to his ear.

"Fifteen minutes," Starling says. "Keep it cool. Don't make a scene. I'll give you a five-minute warning."

"Got it." Phoenix straightens his jacket as we step through to the dining room, his eyes scouring the place, no doubt looking for Raven.

This is about to be the longest fifteen minutes of our lives.

# raven

Jimmy escorts me down the hall, his hand tight on my arm for a bit until we catch up with a few people. That's when he changes his entire demeanor. He's sweet and loving, but his hand is still tight on my waist as he pulls me into the dining hall and escorts me to the head table.

My eyes dart around the room, looking for the guys, hopeful that they're ready to take me away. When I catch sight of them sitting down at a table in the back, with their eyes glued to me, I let out a shaky breath and square my shoulders.

The urge to run to them is overwhelming, but until I can get the shock collar remote out of Jimmy's pocket, the risk of getting hurt is too much right now. Especially in front of a crowd of people who would gladly hand me back over to him.

*We have a plan*, Phoenix signs. *Soon, Red.*

I nod and reach up, quickly swiping away a tear that's trying to escape down my cheek.

Jimmy grins when he pulls out a chair, then brushes my hair behind my shoulders and presses his lips to my ear. "I can't wait for them to watch me touch what's rightfully mine." He kisses my cheek, and I keep my eyes pinned on my guys.

They're my safe space, and I'll get lost in their existence while I wait out whatever plan they have.

"Welcome all," Maxwell says as he stands with a glass of beer in his hand. "I'd like to formally announce the engagement of my daughter, Raven Marie Langston, to my half-son, Jimmy Perkins. They'll both take on the Langston name after the wedding next weekend, of course." He turns toward us and smiles like I imagine a proud father would. "I'm so glad you've found each other and can't wait to hand over the keys to the kingdom."

The crowd cheers, claps, and congratulates us.

Jimmy accepts it all with a smile on his face, saying how excited we are.

My eyes lock on Pierce's from across the room.

*I'll rip his balls off for you, little bird,* he signs.

I lift my drink and cover my trembling lips, not wanting to get caught laughing.

"Enjoy the dinner, and we hope you'll come back next weekend to help celebrate their nuptials." Maxwell sits back down next to Jimmy, leans over, and whispers something in his ear.

Jimmy's hand lands on my thigh under the table, tightening when I jump. He looks over at me and shoves his hand in the pocket with the remote as he nods in response to whatever Maxwell says to him.

I grab a small pen and a napkin and write a message before handing it to Jimmy.

*I need to use the restroom.*

"I'll escort you, *wife.*" He excuses himself from the table and pulls my chair back before grabbing my hand and kissing my knuckles. He's got a hard-on for showing off, and the crowd around us rewards him with their smiles and approving comments.

*Shock collar on my neck. Going to get it off. Back soon,* I sign to the boys.

Pretty sure River was about to be the one to bolt over here. As it is, his knee is bouncing a million times a second and Pierce has to grab his thigh to stop him from moving.

Phoenix nods once and signs, *Be careful, Red.*

"I don't know what you four are saying to each other right now," Jimmy snaps as he pulls me out of the dining hall, "but I don't like being kept out of the loop, *wife.*"

I shake my head and shrug, attempting to look confused.

"Did you even need to use the bathroom? What are you trying to do? Are they here to fuck what's mine?" He pushes me into a nearby office and slams the door shut behind him, then shoves me to my knees. "I want you to go in there with the feeling of my cum sliding down your throat. Remind you exactly who you fucking belong to."

My eyes bulge and I shake my head frantically, unable to communicate the moment he wraps my wrists in one of his hands while he unbuckles his pants with the other. I watch as his pants fall to the floor, and the remote bounces out of his pocket need onto the floor.

"Put my dick in your mouth, Raven, and maybe we'll invite your playthings to the wedding to see you in a pretty dress." He grins as he looks down at me, cupping my face with his free hand. "If you do a good job, I might even let them live."

I look between his dick and the remote on the floor, and with resignation heavy in my chest, I place my mouth over the head and begin distracting him.

"Oh, fuuuck," he groans. He releases my wrists in favor of wrapping my hair in his fist, and tosses his head back when I bring my hands up to wrap around his shaft. "Too big for just one, huh, baby?"

I roll my eyes and shift closer to him, unfortunately shoving his dick further down my throat. But I need the fucking remote.

As I continue to work Jimmy over, promising myself to down an entire bottle of mouthwash later, I slide one hand down his leg and toward his pants.

He's too in the moment to care what else I'm doing.

"Just like that," he groans, tightening his hand in my hair. "I'm gonna—"

The door swings open and slams against the wall, revealing Pierce, River, and Phoenix in all their glory.

"What the fuck?" Jimmy snaps, spinning and pulling his dick from my mouth. He reaches down to grab his pants, and I quickly grab the remote before he has time to see it lying on the floor.

I'm shaking. My hands are trembling.

My body is giving out on me.

I've been in survival mode for so long, and I know I have about two point five seconds before I dissolve into a mess on the floor.

I ignore the shouting, the fists pounding, in favor of stripping the key from the back of the remote. The shock collar is hard to turn, but I get the lock in front of my throat and stick the key in.

Phoenix kneels in front of me as River and Pierce knock Jimmy out and toss him on the couch. "Can I help you, Red?"

I meet his beautiful brown eyes, and his gorgeous face, and nod once before shock takes over.

They're not really here. This is a dream and I'll wake up on the bed in the basement again with Jimmy wrapped around me.

But what a beautiful dream it is.

I reach up and place my hand over his face. My fingers tremble so hard.

"We're here, sweet girl," River croons from my left.

"You're almost free, little bird," Pierce says as he kneels on my right.

"We've got you," Phoenix says as he pulls the shock collar from my neck and glares at it. He grabs the remote and puts them both in his pocket. When I raise a brow, he shakes his head. "Not now, Red. Let's get you out of here."

"Starling gave the signal a few minutes ago," Pierce says to the room. He looks like he wants to pull me in his arms, but forces himself to stand and pull a gun from his suit jacket.

*Guns?* I sign.

"You worry about holding onto me, baby girl, and we'll take care of the rest, okay?" Phoenix pulls me to a stand, then lifts me in his arms, adjusting me into a bridal carry as River and Pierce step in front of the door.

The three of them exchange looks. Pierce holds his fingers against his ear, nods, and meets my gaze.

I don't like what I find in his.

"I love you, Blue," he says before pushing through the door.

Just as the telltale sound of sirens go off, red and blue lights penetrate the windows, and a booming voice sounds over a megaphone.

"FBI! NOBODY FUCKING MOVE!"

My heart rate spikes, and I cling to Phoenix as he follows Pierce and River out of the cabin.

Maxwell's orders are loud and clear, the first one being to find me and Jimmy.

But the guys must have cleared the way before coming, because the hall they rush down is devoid of anyone aside from us.

"You're almost free, Red," Phoenix shouts in my ear as we turn down another corridor and an FBI agent opens the door at the end.

A woman steps in front of it, arms crossed and defiant. I almost don't realize who it is at first, too delirious and filled with adrenaline to understand what's happening. But while she stares at Pierce and her tears fall as he points his gun at her, I feel a pang in my chest for Chloe Jackson.

"PJ," she whispers. "I can't... let you take her."

"Fuck off, Chloe," Pierce snaps as he continues to move toward her. Unafraid. Uncaring.

"I did all of this for you, son," she says. She bravely–or stupidly–grabs his arm and stares into his eyes. "We would have had enough money to leave this state. Get away from it all."

She's sobbing now, her hands trembling and bringing the barrel of the gun closer to her head.

Pierce shakes his head, hits the side of hers with the butt of the gun and sends her sprawling on the floor. "Leave her here," he orders the FBI agent. "She deserves the fate the rest of these assholes get."

"Got it," the agent replies. "Agent Starling has the SUV waiting for you, sir."

Pierce nods and pushes through the door, shoulders bunched high and not a single look back for the woman who birthed him.

As soon as we exit the cabin, the fresh night air rolls through my lungs, and it's as if I go into shock.

I can't think.

I can't really see.

I can only hold on for dear fucking life as the men I love carry me to safety.

I hardly remember them running down a small hill toward a black SUV, much less Phoenix pulling me into his lap and whispering reassurances in my ear as I switch between panic and dissociation.

What I'm sure I make up in my head, though, are the whispered words that come from me, forcing the other three to a stunned silence.

"I missed you."

It's a nice thought, though, and it makes me smile as I drift into a restless sleep in the back seat with Phoenix's hands holding me tight to him.

# CHAPTER ELEVEN

Never in my life have I wanted so badly to hurt someone.

Not Lexi.

Not Xavier.

Not Whitaker.

No one.

When Starling gave us the go ahead to grab our girl, I thought my soul was vibrating out of my body with rage. All I saw was red. The red of her hair, the red of her lipstick, but mostly, the red of the blood I wanted to spill from Jimmy's body as he stuffed his dick down our girl's throat.

Fuck, I'm still mad about it.

The anger has only barely weaned over the last eight hours. It's fucking three in the morning, and all any of us can do is stare at Raven's sleeping form, spread across the king-sized bed in the middle of the penthouse suite in the hotel.

We're only thirty minutes from the cabin, but we

wanted to get her cleaned and comfortable before we went back home.

"I'm exhausted," River mutters from the other end of the bed. He's sitting in one of the chairs we brought in from the dining room, foot over his opposite knee.

"Get some sleep," Pierce says, then yawns and shakes his head. "I'll keep watch over her."

"She's not going anywhere," I tell them both, though I doubt I'll sleep for a century. Keeping her in my line of sight is priority number one.

We fall into silence again, and a few minutes go by before she shifts, a soft, barely there groan escaping her.

"So... we didn't just make shit up when she spoke earlier?" Pierce asks, leaning over the bed and brushing a hair from in front of her face.

We look like crazed stalkers right now.

"I feel like I've made the whole day up." River grins as his eyes fall shut and his head lolls off to the side. He yawns and his grin grows. "It's nice though."

"What I would give to hear you sing for me again, little bird," Pierce whispers. He leans in and kisses her cheek softly.

Unfortunately, the moment Raven realized she was safe earlier, her entire body fought us at every stage. She kicked, punched, scratched, and I don't think she knew she was doing any of it.

She's made small noises since, little groans here and there, but I don't think even she knows it's happening.

But fuck...

Her whispered "I missed you" sounded angelic in the moment.

Still don't think it happened, but with each tiny noise she makes, it brings that moment closer to reality.

"What would have done it?" I ask.

"I've done some research since Thanksgiving," Pierce says. He sighs when Raven smacks his hand away in her sleep and curls in on herself, pulling the blanket over her for protection. Shaking his head, he leans back and sips from the beer in his free hand. "Honestly, she's been fighting so much the last two weeks. I wonder if she put up so many walls, that when the relief of seeing us and knowing she was finally safe came crashing together... it took all those walls down, plus some."

"Mmm." I nod a few times as I watch her frame tremble from another nightmare.

Number four.

I wish with my whole heart that I could crawl into bed with her and wrap my arms around her body, but because trauma sucks and I don't want to make it worse for her, I sit on this chair, and the guys sit on theirs.

Watching her.

Waiting.

"You didn't punch Jimmy enough."

Pierce snorts and grins as he sips his beer. "I wanted to castrate him, but my main focus was getting her the hell out of there."

I nod. "Whitaker was there."

His lips tighten, and he looks over at River. "His dad, too. We should have blown the cabin up."

"Yeah, I don't think that would have worked. Besides," I add, resting my elbows on my knees and leaning forward. "Any revenge we take should be led by her." I nod toward

Raven. "They hurt her in so many ways, and not just over the last two weeks."

"Mostly over the last two weeks," Pierce grunts, glaring at her leg as she slips it out of the blanket.

She's bruised all over. Head to fucking toe. The moment we got her in the shower and she began scrubbing herself raw, Pierce lost his shit.

Surprised we didn't get kicked out of the hotel, honestly.

The table is still broken. The couch torn apart. And, to add insult to injury, he broke the TV so we've been stuck in silence.

"Death would be too merciful," I whisper.

"I'm going to do some research on how we should help with the strength of her voice." Pierce stands and walks over to where our phones have been sitting in a pile on the dresser.

"Let's not push her."

When he looks at me, doubt and insecurity bleed through his expression, and my heart squeezes in my chest.

He knows what she sounds like, and he's aching to hear her again.

"I just want to be ready with options. That's all." He turns back to his phone, and it lights up his face as he goes to work.

Settling myself back in the chair, I smile when Raven stuffs her other leg out from under the blanket and a small, satisfied groan escapes her when the cool air hits her heated skin.

Maybe we aren't dreaming after all.

"RAE! IT'S ME! HEY!" Pierce catches her wrist before she can punch him again, wincing when her other hand makes contact. "Baby, please. It's me."

Her screams are so soft, I don't think even she hears them, but they're there.

And while we're excited about that fact, we're more concerned with the way she's trembling, lashing out, and curling in on herself.

"C'mon, pup," River says. He reaches out and pulls Pierce back a few steps.

Chest heaving, and fresh tears springing to the surface, Pierce nods and leans back against River.

We watch Raven struggle with her surroundings, eyes wide with pure panic.

"Breathe, Red," I order calmly.

Her eyes latch onto mine and her brows furrow in confusion.

"In for four."

Confused and disoriented, she still knows the drill. She inhales for four seconds.

"Hold for four."

Her chest stills as she does.

"Out for four."

It's shaky, but she lets it go.

"Good girl," I praise her. "Again."

She nods and repeats the process three times. The longer she does this, the calmer she becomes, and the more the tension in the room eases. Her eyes fill with tears as she looks between the three of us, then she collapses in a heap in the corner of the room and just sobs.

We all take a step toward her, but I raise my hand to hold the others back.

"Red?" I take a shaky breath.

"Sweet girl, we really need to know how to help you," River says, voice dripping with nervousness.

Pierce says nothing as we stand there and watch her shoulders shake.

She clenches her fists over and over, pulls at her clothes, and attempts to make herself as small as possible.

No one moves for what seems like an eternity, and then she looks up at us all and touches her throat.

"Why can I talk?" she whispers. Her eyes widen in shock, as if she didn't believe it would work.

"I looked up a lot last night," Pierce says. "It seems like all the walls you had put up to protect yourself while at the cabin... well... when they came down... it must have taken down whatever block you had between you and talking."

She tries to speak again, but winces and grips her throat. She goes to sign something, but Pierce kneels in front of her and meets her gaze.

"It's going to hurt. It's been an unused muscle for so long, baby, but you can work it out like anything else. The trauma may still be there, but whatever the block was?" He reaches for her hands, his smile growing when she holds his back. "That block is gone, Blue."

Tears spill down her cheeks and she smiles so bright, I'm convinced I've never seen her smile before.

"No rush, sweet girl," River says as he kneels next to Pierce.

I take a page from their book and sit on the floor with my legs crossed, only a foot of space between us.

We're cornering her, yet she's no longer fighting us or flinching.

Baby steps.

*Can we go home now?* she signs.

Pierce lifts her hand and kisses her knuckles. "Yeah, little bird. We can go home."

# raven

"Things are a little different inside, Blue."

Shifting in my spot between Phoenix and River, I meet Pierce's eyes in the rearview mirror. He knows I hate change, so he's giving me a heads up.

The boys talked about so much on the drive down here. Filling me in on the shed they rebuilt to house Mark and Tris, the progress made on the antidrug, and the state of our school.

They shut Cobalt University down a few days ago, pending further investigation from the FBI. Dorms were closed and students told to leave the campus while they continued their search for me. Granted, half of those agents are under Maxwell's thumb, so it was all for appearances at the end of the day.

"Tris is going to be so excited to see you," River says. He squeezes my thigh and grins when I meet his gaze.

I've flinched a few times over the past two hours, but my heart and soul know these men love me, even if my brain wants to play tricks on me. River's shoulder is warm against my cheek as I lean on it, wrapping my arm around his while holding Phoenix's hand with my free hand.

Pierce runs his thumb along my ankle, having begged me to rest my foot on the center console thirty minutes ago. He turns his head and my heart stutters in my chest at the adoring look in his eyes. "Almost home, Blue."

*Home.*

So many things have happened since the last time this place really felt like home. Between Lexi trying to kill Phoenix and me, and everything on our road trip, I'm worried I won't feel safe anymore.

Looking between my men, I let out a long breath and clear my throat. "Home," I whisper.

A year and a half is a long time to not talk, so even the tiny whispers I've let out have felt like swallowing sandpaper, but fuck, I'm determined to speak normally again.

Whatever this new version of normal is going to be.

"I need a nap," Lance says as we drive through the heavily guarded gates of Junk. Two men on each side watch our vehicle enter, and another two on the inside work to close it.

What the fuck?

"Why?" I whisper.

"We'll explain later," Phoenix says with a soft squeeze to my hand.

I raise an eyebrow at him, and he kisses it, as if to banish all of my skepticism with his love.

I'll let him do it. For now.

Junk hasn't changed much since we were here last, except for the vegetables growing in the garden, and Mark and Tris' shed. There's also security everywhere, and an RV parked in an empty space to the left of that.

A tall man with a deep scowl, muscles for days, and a head full of messy hair comes storming out of it. He crosses his arms and glares at the vehicle, then follows us toward the garage.

I try to whisper, to ask who that person is, but when the pain becomes too much, I rest my head back on River's shoulder. *Who's that?* I sign.

"One of Lance's guys," Pierce answers. "Actually, it would be Starling's now, right?"

Lance shrugs. "No idea right now. If we go forward with that particular plan, we're going to make some quick enemies of the government."

"You're already on their radar," Phoenix says.

Another shrug from Lance. "We're more concerned with getting you guys safe right now."

Pierce jumps out of the Jeep the second Lance puts it in park, then River and Phoenix follow suit.

As I climb out of the back seat, with the help of those I love, a crowd forms just outside the garage. Mark, Tris, Lance. A bunch of people I don't know dressed in various tactical gear. It's overwhelming, but I know each and every one of them had a hand in saving my life yesterday.

Tears roll down my cheeks as I lift my hand, sign, and say, "Thank you," as clear as I can manage.

Then, applause.

And hugs.

So many hugs.

I don't get as jumpy or scared as much as I thought I would, though all of my guys are on edge and each of them has either a hand or an eye on me at all times. Never in my wildest dreams would I think I'd have been worth all of this effort.

All of this love.

"Rae!" Tris squeals as she pushes her way toward me. Her complexion and overall demeanor are so much healthier than when I last saw her. She wraps her arms around me and squeezes a little too hard, but I don't mind.

"Hey," I whisper, and she pulls back.

Eyes wide and mouth hung open, she takes a moment to assess this new development.

"Tris," Mark says as he places his arm on her shoulder. "It's time to go and let everyone get some rest, okay?"

With a playful roll of her eyes, Tris smiles and hugs me one more time. "We have so much to talk about. But yes," she says, nodding, "please get some rest."

I nod and am about to turn back to my guys when Agent Starling turns toward me with his phone in his hand and a deep frown marring his features.

Immediately, I shake my head. I don't want to know what's going on. I don't need more bad news.

I just don't.

He clears his throat, and I hold up my hand, but he sighs and looks over my shoulder. "We need to have a talk."

Instead of going inside, taking a long bath, and curling up with my boys, I follow everyone inside with my fingers clutched tightly to the hem of the hoodie I'm wearing. My knuckles turn white, and my fingers shake, but it's better than focusing on the tense emotions surrounding me.

I knew I was dreaming earlier.

"Here," Phoenix says, handing over a warm tumbler. "Take a few sips. Fix your breathing. We'll wait for your signal on this one, Red."

I nod and do as he says. Warmth travels down my throat

along with the hot cocoa and I groan softly, making every man in the room turn to stare at me.

No one had me getting my voice back on their bingo card. That's for sure. Not even me.

Pierce sits on my left and clutches my free hand between his, sliding his thumbs on my skin as if he's trying to remember everything. He reacquaints himself with my features. It's distracting and calming, and when River sits on his other side and places his hand on ours, I can't help the smile that breaks across my face.

Phoenix sits on my other side and leans forward, planting his elbows on his knees. He glares across the coffee table at Agent Starling, who's watching us with a tense expression.

His lips curve up into a smile, but it's his eyes that tell us something is incredibly, terribly wrong.

I take a deep breath and nod once. Ready or not, the spell is going to break.

"Spit it out," Pierce snaps when the older man takes too long to speak.

His hands shake as he leans forward, and he folds them together as he meets my eyes. "They let Maxwell out this morning."

"What?" Pierce roars. He pushes my hand out of his lap and launches toward Starling, but River grabs him to hold him back.

"Calm down," River tells him, calmly.

Phoenix just stares at the floor, nodding, and I look between everyone in complete and utter shock.

I pull my phone out and text our group chat, because I don't trust myself to even attempt to speak right now.

Who the hell got him out? Why does he get a free pass? How do we get him back in custody? And if these people are all in the FBI, why the hell is this even happening?

"Rae," Phoenix sighs, stuffing his phone in his pocket. He turns toward me, and the defeat in his eyes hurts. "Every single person working with us over the last few weeks…"

"We've all been fired," Starling finishes for him.

"Wait, what?" Phoenix asks, turning his gaze back to him.

River wrangles Pierce back on the couch and they both sit next to me again.

Defeated, exhausted, and beaten, Starling sits back in the chair and nods. "I was fired, and am currently under investigation."

"Holy shit," River says, slumping back against the couch. "How far does this go?"

Starling shakes his head and twists his mustache.

We sit there in silence for so long, the sound of the wind becomes the only constant. It reminds us that we're here. We're alive. We're okay.

But for how long?

"I'm going to go inform the team," Starling says, standing and brushing off his pants. "I have to get back to headquarters before they formally arrest me tomorrow morning."

The guys all stand and shake his hand one by one. When Pierce reaches out for a hug, I think everyone is shocked.

"You helped bring my girl back. We'll help make this right for you."

With a shake of his head, Starling pats Pierce on the back and grins at me. "I've had backup plans for my backup plans, kids. Don't worry about me. You get yourselves together."

"What do we do about Maxwell?" Phoenix asks.

With an evil glint in his eye, Starling simply shrugs and walks out into the garage.

Pierce kicks the coffee table and slides his hands through his hair, messing it up more than it already was. "I'm going to kill every motherfucker who's ever worked with Langston."

"Alright, pup," River says, patting him on the back. "Can we do it after a nap?"

I can't help it. I laugh. And because it finally carries sound with it, all the guys look over at me. Their expressions are such a mix of confusion and shock and admiration that I laugh a little harder.

It's not loud by any means, but it breaks the small fraction of tension left. I'm reminded that even though we're still stuck in the darkest times of our lives, the light can break through.

We just have to let it.

# *pierce*

I never really could sleep when Rae was in my arms. Not fully. Anytime she curled up in my arms when we were younger, I'd stay awake and watch her. Then down all the caffeine imaginable so I could keep up with her on whatever new adventure she wanted us to go on the next day.

I'd do anything for her.

So, while I watch her sleep in the middle of the massive bed we installed up here, wrapped around Phoenix and River, I plot.

I plan.

Think.

Rethink.

Consume three energy drinks.

A few cups of coffee.

I drown out the entire world with the sounds of her soft snores, mixed with the clicking of my fingers on the keyboard and my pencil scribbling on paper.

Back in Florida, we made a plan to lure them all to the spot where it all began. I said we could blow them all up.

Everyone thought it was a good idea, but also a bad idea. If we lure them into the science lab at CU... we have to get out before it blows. But we all know that Maxwell won't let us leave.

So, while I plan, I stare at my crew and know that I'll be the one to leave that room last.

Hell, Rae won't enter it at all.

The alarm on my phone goes off, lighting up the room with sound and forcing a groan from everyone. Except me. I turn it off, and smile when Rae climbs out of the bed and makes her way toward me.

"Good morning, little bird," I whisper.

She goes to lift her hands, then smiles shyly as she drops them by her side again. "Good morning," she whispers.

"Fucking hell." I reach out, grab her waist, and pull her down to straddle my lap. I breathe in the fresh smell of strawberry soda she bathed in last night, and rest my chin on her shoulder. "I thought the world was ending without you."

Red hair tumbles around her shoulders and covers my hands as she shakes her head. When she pulls back, her eyes are full of tears, but she's still smiling. "We have," she clears her throat, "too much life left, G-Green."

"Hey," I say, gripping her chin and keeping our gazes locked. "Don't force yourself to talk if it hurts, okay? Hell, if you never want to talk another day in your life, you don't have to."

"But—" she whispers, then winces.

In all the research I did, I learned that it would take weeks for her voice to get strong. It's an unused muscle, after all. So while I'll work with her on it, I know it's going to be a lot to deal with.

And we've already dealt with enough for now.

"Can I kiss you?" I ask, instead of starting an argument.

Progress.

She doesn't hesitate. Not one millisecond. She places her hands on my shoulders, leans forward, and presses her lips to mine.

My entire body surges back to life. I'm no longer drowning. No longer locked inside a cage without her. The cage doesn't exist. We're free. Flying. Existing with each other the way we did as kids.

Only now, my cock hardens in my sweats as she squirms in my lap, seeking friction and closeness. Connection.

Love.

She moans. It's soft. Barely noticeable. But fuck if it isn't the sweetest sound.

I could cry.

I peek over her shoulder at Phoenix and River, still asleep on the bed, and stand, lifting Rae into my arms. "Do you need me, little bird?"

She nods, wrapping her legs around my waist and her arms around my neck as I carry her down the stairs.

Light shines into the living room, a beam showcasing the couch, which is exactly where I lay her down. Her skin glows, and her eyes twinkle.

"You're so fucking beautiful." I lean over her and drag Phoenix's t-shirt off her, exposing her breasts and underwear to me. With my eyes locked on hers, I lick a path around her nipple and slide my fingers beneath her waistband before pulling her underwear all the way down her legs.

Her back arches, and my dick weeps.

I catch sight of a few bruises along her hips and legs, and kiss them each away as I make my way down her body. Once she's naked, I simply stroke my hands along her skin, feeling her.

She's safe.

She's here.

She's everything.

"I'm so sorry," I tell her. She winces when my fingers touch a nasty bruise, so I kiss that, too. "I'm so, so sorry."

She shakes her head and wipes away a tear before gripping my face with both hands and glaring at me, a mix of playfulness and sadness in her eyes. "Not your fault."

"But—"

Her fingers smash against my lips as she stops me from talking, and she shakes her head again. "R-Replace the memories," she whispers.

I reach out and pull a strand of hair sticking to her lips and nod. I'll do anything she asks for the rest of our lives. I kiss the side of her neck where another bruise sits, then make my way down her body again until my lips are barely above where she wants me most.

One kiss to her left thigh.

Another to her right.

A last one just above her clit that makes her back arch and her hips chasing me for more.

A dark chuckle rolls through me as I wrap my arms around her legs and meet her gaze. "Needy much?"

She rolls her eyes, and I nip at her thigh in retaliation. She glares.

"Be a good girl, Rae, and I'll let you come." I wink when

she narrows her eyes, then dive right in and devour her. My favorite fucking meal. I'd starve without her.

With each new swipe of my tongue, she arches. She pulls my hair, forcing me closer. She cries out when I suck on her clit.

I stuff three fingers in her a little too rough, but the pain makes her gasp and I smirk before diving back in.

Her heels dig into the couch beside me, and I place my free hand on her stomach, holding her down. I keep my eyes firmly on her face as it contorts in that gorgeous pleasure-pain she so often finds herself in with me. Just as I'm sure I'm about to come in my damn sweats, her entire body freezes, and I keep going. I keep fucking her with my fingers, my mouth, my tongue. I draw out every last drop of her as she comes undone beneath me, and when she thinks she's done, I keep going.

I don't let up until she's coming again and tears are falling down her face.

She tries to push me away again, and this time, I let her.

I only go so far, though. I take off my sweats and pull her close to me, spreading her legs with my thighs. Eyes still on her face, hands still massaging her skin. "I love watching you fly for me, little bird."

She grins. It's lazy and adorable, and her eyes hardly open. Her hands slide up and down my forearms and send tingles up my spine.

I shiver, and she giggles.

"Fuck, I missed that sound." I press my lips to hers and kiss her lazily for a few seconds. "I want to fuck you so bad, Rae. Tell me not to."

She shakes her head and kisses her way to my ear. "Make l-love to me, Green."

I press my face into her shoulder and groan. My dick twitches as she moves herself underneath me, connecting us just enough I can feel how soaked she is for me. "Are you okay?"

She nods and slides her fingers into my hair, pulling me closer to her. Her heels dig into my ass as she pulls me closer. Closer.

With a deep breath, I enter her pussy gently. Not unlike the first time I did this with her. I make love to her, instead of fucking her. I'm soothing instead of hating. Loving. Adoring.

My entire world stops and ends with this woman, and I know, without a doubt, that we'll get through the pain and heartache and trials and tribulations.

So long as we have each other, all will be right with the world.

Sweat rolls down my body as I hold on to all of my restraint, fisting the ends of the couch so I don't pound into her the way I want to. But when I pull back and see her staring up at me, I can't help but grab her face in my hands and kiss her.

Sparks fly, and I move faster.

She moans, and I chase the sound.

I keep going and going, and with each thrust, I become a little more forceful.

"I can't… I can't hold back with you, Blue," I breathe. "Ever."

"Don't," she whispers before pulling me into her further, nails scratching along my back.

I nod and kiss her roughly. Teeth nipping at her lower lip, creating bite marks I know are *mine* and not his.

Bruise her hips with my hands.

Mark her insides, claiming her for us. Not anyone else.

"Come for me again," I command in her ear before biting down on her earlobe. I growl when she contracts around me, squeezing the life out of me. "Come, little bird."

Seconds later, she lets out a shrill little scream that wakes Phoenix and River, and I come inside of her, pumping my hips until there's nothing left to give her.

Then I laugh.

And cry.

And kiss her.

And Phoenix and River glare over the railing at both of us, and Rae laughs.

As I lay down on top of her to catch my breath and my cum leaks out of her, even that becomes funny and we're all laughing again like we were last night.

We all feel it.

The shift.

"Here we were respecting your boundaries, little vixen," River says as he walks down the stairs, "and we find you sticky, sweaty, and full of cum already." He shakes his head and kisses her lips before smacking my ass and walking to the kitchen. "I call dibs next."

"Really, River?" Phoenix raises a brow as he looks at all of us, then shakes his head. He walks over and kisses Raven's forehead. "Shower with me?"

She nods and wiggles her body, freeing herself from the couch.

Phoenix tosses her over his shoulder and laughs when she does. "I'll make breakfast when I'm done welcoming Red back home."

"Hey!" River shouts, rushing toward the stairs, but he's too late.

Phoenix enters the bathroom with Rae, then slams and locks the door before River even makes it to the top stair.

I lay back on the couch, smiling as I watch the sunrise over the fence.

Happy.

Content.

Loved.

The rest of the world can wait.

CHAPTER FOURTEEN

# raven

Phoenix slams the door and places me directly in the middle of the shower.

Sweat coats my body. Pierce's cum is still leaking from me, sliding down my thighs and reminding me of the man who somehow ruthlessly fucked and made love to me at the same time.

"Good morning, Red," Phoenix says. A little too sweet, seeing as he's glaring at me and smiling at the same time.

"Morning," I whisper. It's easy to whisper, so I'll stick to that for now.

"We were all going to wait patiently. We really were. But if you're good..." he trails off as he strips his clothes off and steps into the shower.

The water comes out cold at first, pulling a shriek from my throat as I back into the tiles to escape it. But I groan as it warms up and Phoenix pulls me under the showerhead.

He wraps his hand in my hair and slams his lips to mine. His hard cock nestles against my stomach as he holds me there.

I explore his body, hands trailing across his shoulders, down his arms, down his sides. My nails score up his abs and chest until I reach up and wrap my hands in his hair, pulling it free of his bun and letting his strands fall down his shoulders.

Brown eyes meet mine as he breaks the kiss, and the adoring expression in them makes my heart skip a few beats as I fall harder for him.

We're smiling like idiots at each other, but I don't care.

"I missed you, Red. We all did. Those idiots at least had each other to keep their dicks warm, though."

I glance down at him, and my eyes widen when I take in the metal bar that now adorns it.

He laughs at the shock on my face and places his fingers underneath my chin. "Had to feel something down there. Why not more pain?"

I bite my lip as I reach out to feel the piercing he now has, surprised by the instant lust that covers his face when I play with it. The man gave me more power with that piercing than he planned. As I play with it more, his hands tremble, and when I glance down, I watch as a bead of pre-cum drops onto my hand.

"Get on your knees, Red."

Pretty sure I hurt myself on the way down, but I don't care. I'm curious.

And curiosity satiates the pussy, right?

Phoenix grips my hair in one hand and opens my jaw with the other. He thrusts his thumb in my mouth and watches me with heavy-lidded eyes as I suck on it, forcing a groan from him. "Good girl."

I clench my thighs together and close my eyes. Fuck, I missed him calling me that.

"Open your eyes and watch as I stuff my cock down your throat, Raven."

I reach out and wrap my hand around his shaft, and wrap my lips around him. He thrusts forward, and I only take him deeper, allowing spit to coat him and my tears to spring free.

The metal from his piercing slides along my tongue and I flick it, testing the waters with what it does for him.

His knees tremble and he holds onto my hair tighter.

I grin.

"Such a good little slut. Do you like it?" His eyes lock on mine. Questioning. Vulnerable.

I nod and suck him deeper, both of us groaning when my nose presses against his lower stomach and I can no longer breathe.

"Should make you stay like this. Make up all the time we've missed, huh?" His fingers gently massage my scalp as he talks like this, soothing. Comforting. Cherishing me.

He pulls back and looks down at me, pressing his hand to my cheek and pulling out slowly before pushing back in. He watches me like a hawk as he fucks my throat and groans when I simply let him use me.

Because at the end of the day, the only people who I'll ever give this much control to will be these men.

Phoenix loses control after a few more thrusts and holds my head in both hands as he fucks my face.

I could die like this. Happily.

I groan, allowing the vibrations to travel along his dick and grip his thighs as his knees threaten to buckle.

"Fuck," he breathes. "Do that again."

So I do.

"I'm gonna—"

He doesn't get the word out, but I feel it as he shoots down my throat, claiming me like Pierce did. His hips stutter until he stills, and he looks down at me with only love in his gaze as I swallow.

For a few moments, as he softens and catches his breath, we simply stare at each other, though I'm sure I don't look as pretty as he claims.

"Alright," he says, pulling out of my mouth and helping me to my feet. "Let's get cleaned. Then you can have a proper breakfast."

"THERE SHE IS!" River says as I round the corner, hand locked in Phoenix's. "You're fucking rude, Nixy boy. Took her right from under me!"

"Actually," Pierce says around a mouthful of toast, "she was literally under me."

"Whatever," River says, waving him away. He wraps me in his arms and twirls me around. "I missed you, sweet girl."

"Put her down and let her eat," Phoenix tells him.

River sighs and does as he's told, placing me on a stool. He goes around the counter and pulls a plate out of the oven. A big goofy grin stretches his lips as he sets it in front of me.

I dig into the food while the guys chatter about nothing, and River turns on music, which makes me smile.

It reminds me of all the times spent dancing with him.

I fucking missed everything about being here.

"How sore are you?" River asks as he sits down next to me.

*Not at all*, I sign as I take another bite of food.

"Good," he says, pushing my now empty plate across the counter. "Then you wouldn't mind bending over the counter while I—"

Someone pounds their fist against the door, hard.

River tosses his head back and groans. He turns his head and glares at Phoenix. "You! You took my chance!"

"It's not like you weren't getting your dick wet the whole time she was gone." Phoenix rolls his eyes and puts his coffee down on the way to the door. He opens it to reveal Mark and Tris.

Mark looks frazzled, his hair sticking every which way and eyes wide with panic.

It's Tris I'm most concerned with, though.

Her eyes fill with tears as our gazes meet, and she rushes toward me when I stand from the counter. "Oh, Rae. I'm so, so sorry. I didn't realize it'd be our fault that he'd—"

"Hey," I whisper, pulling back to peer into her eyes. "It's okay."

"You what?" Pierce roars, and I jerk back, turning to the door where all the men have gathered. "Why the fuck would you do that?"

"I just... I thought... well..."

"Get the hell off of my property," Pierce shouts at him, pushing him out of the door. "Go."

"Hold on a second," Phoenix says, pushing Pierce back a few steps. "Let's listen to what he has to say. We'll figure it out from there. River, call Lance."

"Got it," River says. He grabs his phone from the counter and does just that.

"What the fuck were you thinking?" Pierce snaps at Mark again.

"I-I—"

"You fucking weren't!" Pierce tosses his hands in the air and turns around, frustration and devastation written all over his face. "I knew bringing you onto my property was a bad idea. I knew it, and when I told everyone else, not a single person thought different."

"Pierce—" Phoenix tries to calm him, but only gets shoved against the wall.

"Hey!" I shout, a little too quietly, but Pierce's gaze snaps my way. "Stop being an asshole." I point between all of them. "Sit down." I point to the couch.

Defeated, although I don't know why, Pierce sits down on the couch and shoves his face in his hands.

Mark follows and sits in the chair across from him, where Agent Starling told us about my father being let out of jail last night.

I bring Tris over to sit next to the kitchen island and hand her a bottle of water from the fridge. And because the men in my life don't know how to act like adults, I stand at the end of the coffee table, cross my arms, and stare at Mark.

Lance comes barging in, immediately raking his eyes over Tris multiple times before taking a deep breath. He looks around the room, assessing the situation, and when he sees us all glaring at Mark, he walks over and crosses his arms. "Explain."

"I, uh," Mark starts, then clears his throat. "I went to see Maxwell last night. Try to broker a deal. Something. Let you guys go. Not go for revenge... but..."

"Not the smartest choice there, Riley," Lance says. He sighs and pulls out his phone. "Fuck. I can't even tell Starling about this. They have him in a cell."

"Seriously?" Phoenix turns toward Lance, shocked.

"Yeah. Don't worry about it." Waving off the concern for his sometimes boss, Lance looks at Mark again. "What happened at Langston's?"

"He said he'd let me work for him again if I turned on you guys…"

Pierce snorts. "Of course he did."

"He said Raven has two weeks to come to her senses, or he's sending a team to grab her." Mark's distraught eyes meet mine, sending chills down my spine and warning bells sounding in my head. "By any means necessary. He'd rather have you dead than here."

I swallow harshly and sit down on River's lap, allowing him to wrap his arms around me and pull me close.

"We need to leave," Phoenix says.

"I don't want to hide," Pierce snaps. He stands and paces around the living room.

"We could go back to Rae's…" River hugs me closer to him and rests his head on my shoulder.

Pierce shoots him an incredulous look. "He'd know we were there. He has eyes everywhere in that town."

"So let him," Phoenix snaps, and we all turn to stare at him. "Seriously. Let him watch us live a normal fucking life like he doesn't exist. Then, when he's had enough, he'll come for her."

"We make him believe she's packing up her things. Ready to go to him," Lance chimes in.

Phoenix stares at him for a beat, wheels no doubt turning in his head as he nods slowly. "Then we have him meet us at the school to give her over."

Pierce sighs and rubs the bridge of his nose. "How do we get the rest of his crew there?"

"We could fake some text messages, inviting them to meet. Who's closest to who?" River asks.

The room goes quiet, and Lance nods his head a few times. "Leave that part to us. You guys get your shit and get out of here."

"What about Mark and Tris?" Pierce asks while glaring at the two in question.

"We'll stay here," Mark says. "If Maxwell wants to come for me while you guys are away, I'll be ready."

"If Tris is staying, I'm staying," Lance says. His cheeks turn red when we all stare at him and he clears his throat. "I mean... I'm head of the team, so I should keep eyes on them, anyway. I know the most."

I cover my smile with my hand when I catch sight of Tris's cheeks turning as red as his.

"So... we're just... leaving Junk?" Pierce asks. He looks around the room and sighs.

"We worked hard on this, Pierce," Phoenix says, placing a hand on his shoulder. "But we're gonna do what we have to in order to keep her safe. Let him think what he wants. Besides," he adds, meeting my gaze, "our girl deserves to be free, and locking her up behind a gate isn't that."

Lance stuffs his hands in his pockets and looks around the room. "You've got your original plan. Just tweak it. Whatever you need from my team, they'll be there for you. I'll hold down the fort here."

I stand and walk over to Lance to wrap my arms around him in a tight hug. "Thank you," I whisper.

He chuckles and hugs me back–quickly, so the guys don't get mad–then pulls away and smiles. "We'll get you your freedom from this asshole. I promise."

With that, he walks away, but not before mouthing

something to Tris that causes her blush to grow and Mark to glare at him as he leaves the room.

"Well," River says, clapping his hands on his thighs and standing up. "Guess we're going to prepare for Thanksgiving part three."

Tris's brows furrow in confusion. "What does that mean?"

"Nothing," Phoenix says while shooting a glare at River. "Absolutely nothing."

# river

If anyone would have told me I would have been moving back to a small town, with less than a thousand people, I'd have laughed in their fucking face.

But for RaeRae... I'd do anything.

"Are we there yet?"

Rae giggles in the backseat. I meet her pretty blue eyes in the rearview mirror and wink.

"I swear," Pierce grumbles, tightening his hands on the wheel, "I want to leave you on the side of the fucking road."

"Aw, but then you wouldn't be able to enjoy getting fucked in the ass as much, pup!"

Phoenix snorts and hides it behind a fake scowl, but it's too late. I already saw his smile.

"Rae. Baby." Pierce groans. "Please let me leave him."

"No way," she says softly.

Her voice is so sweet, it's almost impossible to match it with the sass she gives us daily. I'm jealous Pierce ever got to hear her before us.

"But seriously," I say, leaning over and pressing my chin on his shoulder. "Are we there yet?" I whisper.

He plants his palm on the side of my head and pushes me back into my seat. But he laughs.

And that laugh creates a domino effect of laughter in the Jeep until there are tears in everyone's eyes and my stomach hurts.

These are the moments I've loved since Rae's been back.

Doesn't matter how stressed we've been, we're always finding something to laugh about.

I want to give her a lifetime of these moments.

"What the fuck?" Pierce barks, pulling the car off to the side of the road in front of the town sign. "Did I take a wrong turn?"

A sheet covers the sign and a few construction cones surround it.

"Says it's under new ownership," Phoenix says as he leans between the seats to get a better view.

"Who the hell would want to buy this town? No one's given a shit about it before now." Pierce pulls his phone out of the cupholder and starts poking around on the internet. "Grayson Hargraves. Estranged Heir to the Hargraves Estate. Left town five years ago with his pregnant girlfriend. The girlfriend and their daughter died on New Year's Day at one in the morning, after all three were hit by a driver under the influence of..." His eyes meet mine as he swallows. "Someone under the influence of Rapture killed them."

"Does it really say that?" I ask, leaning over to read from his phone.

"No, but it doesn't have to. Says they were high on some new drug." He shakes his head and goes back to reading.

"Looks like he's coming back to get a new purpose in life or some shit. He now owns the town and plans to change the name."

"What's the new name?" Rae whispers.

We look up just as a guy parks his white construction truck next to the sign.

He climbs out and picks up the cones, then tosses them in the bed of his truck. After swiping his hand through his messy brown hair, he reaches up and rips the sheet off the brand new sign.

Welcome to Aurora Falls.

"I like it," Rae says.

I glance at her and smile when our eyes meet. "Not worried about too much change, RaeRae?"

She shakes her head. "This town needs to heal, just like we do."

Pierce presses his lips together in a firm line and puts the Jeep back in gear before getting back on the road. He drives in silence, but the way he white-knuckles the steering wheel tells us everything we need to know.

He does *not* want this change.

It doesn't take long to crest over the last hill and see the valley below. The one we've been to twice now, but only for visits.

This time we're moving. And if Rae never wants to leave again, that's okay with me.

I actually like this little town. It's a bit run-down, but with a guy with a name like Grayson Hargraves, I've got a feeling he's going to fix it up and it'll be better than it ever was.

Even if it is a small town.

I shudder and pull out the last Twizzler from the bag and stuff one end in my mouth to avoid saying things I shouldn't. Like "Let's get the fuck out of here" or "Small towns suck ass and breed assholes".

Not everyone is my father.

"That new guy, Julian," Nix says before he yawns. "He's dropping off the Uhaul, then grabbing a ride back with one of the other guys to the motel."

Pierce nods.

Great. He's not talking.

"We need to get all of their names memorized." I kick my feet up on the dash and watch as we roll through the middle of town, past old shops.

Construction crews are everywhere.

"Once Langston's dead, there won't be a need for all this security," Pierce says. He pulls onto the street he and Rae grew up on, slowing down when he sees a giant red FOR SALE sign outside of his mother's house. His eyes widen as he takes in the sight.

"Pierce," Rae says, leaning forward and placing a hand on his shoulder.

"Good fucking riddance, bitch," he snarls as he turns into Rae's driveway. He doesn't wait for any of us. Simply gets out and storms into the backyard.

A few seconds later, birds go flying out of the trees when he screams.

"Let's go inside," Nix suggests as he gets out, pulling a sad Rae with him. "He'll be okay, Red."

She nods, though her eyes linger in Pierce's direction until she has to unlock the front door and step inside.

I wait outside for Julian and the rest of our crew, and

when they hand me the keys to the Uhaul, I wave them off and make my way to the backyard.

Pierce is sitting on an old swing set, kicking at the dirt as he pushes himself back and forth. His head is in his hands, and his shoulders are shaking.

Fuck.

"Hey, pup."

"Go away," he grumbles, wiping away his tears.

"Don't think I will." I sit on the swing next to his and wrap my arm around his shoulders, pulling him into my side. "It's okay to be sad that she's gone."

"No, it's fucking not. She abused me. She left me for dead most of my fucking life. Now," he laughs, tossing his hands in the air, "she's going to be by his side. She's fully fucking," his voice cracks. "She's fucking going to be with him. The man who has ruined everything." His shoulders shake with his silent cries.

I rest my head on top of his and rub his arm, hoping to comfort him at least a little. "It might not be the same, but I do know what it feels like to watch a mother ignore you like that, pup. To watch a mother not do the basic things a mother should do. To have a mother allow someone to abuse you constantly."

"Maxwell never ab—"

"He did. In a way," I interrupt. "He beat the shit out of you multiple times since you were a teenager, man. He manipulated you in every way possible. All to keep an eye on his daughter. He wants to be the evil villain, yet I bet he can't even do a proper evil villain laugh." I mimic said evil villain laugh, bouncing my shoulders and tossing my head back.

Pierce shakes his head and laughs a watery laugh while

shoving me off of him and readjusting in the swing. "This year has been a lot."

I nod. "It really fucking has, but it's been a fuck ton of good. I met you and Nixy boy. Then we met Rae."

"We treated her like shit," he says.

"Yeah." I shrug. "And we groveled for it. Now we just have to take care of Maxwell Langston and his dastardly crew of evil cronies."

Pierce snorts and rolls his eyes. "You're an idiot."

"Oh, darn," I say, giving him a deadpan look. Like I care. I just want to make him laugh and smile and be happy.

Like I wish someone would have done for me.

He grins and looks out at the trees which hide the abandoned playground he and Rae claimed as their own so many years ago. "We should go unpack. I need some fucking—"

"Me too."

"Sleep, River. I need sleep." He stands and wipes his face with the bottom of his shirt, exposing his delicious abs to the rest of the world.

"Alright," I say, sighing. I wrap my arms around him and press a kiss to his forehead. "I'm here. We're all here. This will all be over in two weeks."

"What the fuck do we do?"

I shrug. "Not a goddamn clue, but I have a feeling we're staying in Aurora Falls."

He groans and plants his forehead against my shoulder. "I don't need more change."

"Ah, but pup." I reach out and lift his chin with my fingers, forcing his eyes to mine. "This is a change for the better, and those changes are absolutely okay."

"If you say so," he grumbles.

"I do." I kiss his lips softly, then pull him back toward

the front of the house. "Now, be a good boy and help me unload the truck."

"Yes, sir," he says with a slight grin. A tinge of pink spreads across his cheeks, but he does as he's told.

Shame. I was looking forward to punishing the stubborn out of him tonight.

## raven

Watching as three hot as shit guys move furniture around should not be as entertaining as it is.

It definitely shouldn't distract me from this book I'm reading, because it's one of my all-time favorites.

I have completely betrayed reader kind by salivating over my boyfriends and sipping a Cherry Coke while I do it.

"Keep staring like that and I'll have to come over there and do something about it," Phoenix says. He grunts as he fixes the new bookcase in place, and his back muscles glisten, distracting me, yet again, from my task in hand.

Fuck reading.

I close the book and place it on the coffee table, then curl my knees up to my chest and hold my can in both hands. My eyes trace every inch of tattooed muscle on Phoenix as I sip leisurely from my straw.

"Seriously," he chuckles, "I can feel your eyes all over me." He turns around and plants his hands on his hips.

Our eyes meet, and I shrug.

"Bed's all set," River says as he walks into the room. Also shirtless.

Pierce walks in behind him and nearly kills me.

"Why are we all staring at Rae?" River asks.

"Because she's gawking at us while we're doing all the hard labor for her," Phoenix replies. He saunters toward me, grabs my Coke, and plops it onto the side table. "Told you I'd do something about it."

I let out a shriek that surprisingly doesn't hurt my throat when he grabs me around the waist and lifts me into his arms. My entire body wraps around him as I hold on for dear life, not knowing where he's taking me, but fuck it, I'll go wherever he is.

"We still have shit to move!" Pierce shouts.

"Don't care," Phoenix shouts back as he marches up the stairs. "Pretty sure Rae's a little thirsty."

I bite my lip and open my eyes as River and Pierce race up the stairs behind us. Only a few seconds pass before Phoenix tosses me onto the bed and descends after me, sliding his sweaty body along my bare legs and arms.

Playful Phoenix is my favorite, and he hasn't had the chance to be like this often enough.

"I'm pretty sure my new favorite sound is your laughter," he says before kissing my shoulder.

I squirm under him, thighs clenching with each new kiss that he peppers along my skin. My body lights up as he removes my t-shirt and shorts, and my heart hammers in my chest as Pierce and River make their way onto the large bed.

Never in my life did I think I'd own a bed this big, but here we are. And we all fit.

Since we spent the entire morning on the road, and most

of the afternoon bringing in our things, well, I'd say we finally get to test it out.

"Wanna play a little, RaeRae?" River asks from my left. His hand is already in his pants, stroking himself.

"Yeah," I breathe. "Hell yeah."

"Ask nicely, Red," Phoenix commands. He pulls my underwear down and tosses them onto the floor.

My body flushes as they stare at me. The bruises caused by Jimmy are almost gone, finally. Some replaced by Pierce, but those are my favorite. Those are the ones that remind me I'm in control.

I chew on my lip as they observe me for a few seconds, then crook my finger at Pierce, beckoning him to me. "Remember Valentine's Day?"

Pierce tosses his head back on a groan and glances over at River, who shrugs.

"You sure you're up for that, Red?" Phoenix asks. He trails his hands to my ass and massages it. "It's been a while."

"I want it."

"Do we even know where the lu—"

"Right here!" River says happily. He leans over and pulls open the bedside table drawer and tosses a bottle of lube, a few toys, and half a dozen other things onto the bed. He looks at us all like a proud little puppy waiting for praise.

"When did you have time to find all that?" Pierce asks, inspecting a few things I can't make out.

"They were on the top of my bag. My top packing priority." River winks and shoves his pants down, revealing his cock, already leaking at the tip.

"Of fucking course it's your priority," Phoenix says. He sighs and massages my thighs as he looks down at me.

"Turn around, hang your head off the end, and spread those pretty legs for us, yeah?"

I nod, and as Phoenix climbs off the bed and strips his pants off, I turn and do as I'm told. Dizziness takes over at first, but by the time my equilibrium is back to normal, River's already got a finger prodding at my ass.

Pierce moves to the other side of me on the bed and trails his hands from the center of my collarbone all the way to my clit and back again. His eyes devour me, and the more I watch him watch me, the more wet I get.

They're teasing.

Taunting.

Playing.

I whimper, and River's hand tightens on my thigh as he spreads me further.

"Fucking hell," Phoenix breathes.

"Lift, sweet girl," River says with a tap on my thigh.

I do, and the men gently caress my body as they maneuver themselves around me.

River underneath.

Pierce on top.

Phoenix biding his time at the end of the bed with his hand stroking through my hair.

I reach out for his dick and stroke it a few times as River and Pierce run their fingers through my wetness, spreading it and lube all over until they're satisfied they won't hurt me.

River enters me slowly, groaning in my ear loud enough that Pierce tightens his hands on my thighs.

Fuck.

"You okay?" Pierce asks, lifting my chin with his fingers until our eyes meet.

"Perfect," I breathe.

He grins and slides the tip of his dick between my folds, then pushes in, watching as every inch sinks home. "God damn. I forgot how tight this was. How fucking perfect we all fit together."

"Hey there, Red," Phoenix says. He leans down and kisses me as the other two slowly move, their shallow thrusts sending me insane. "Open up," he commands, standing and pushing the head of his dick toward my mouth.

I oblige so fast, he chuckles, groaning when I pull him further into me. With my hands firmly on his ass, I take him to the back of my throat. When Pierce and River move, I relax my entire body and allow them to use me.

If I believed in Heaven, this would be it.

My muscles ache in the best ways as their hands roam and pinch, and their dicks stroke every inch of the inside of me. They fill me in every way, and despite that, it's not enough. I reach for River's hand and slide it over my swollen, throbbing clit, and he happily takes the reins, massaging it in firm tight circles. Just the way I like it.

Seconds turn to what feels like hours, and their paces pick up, stutter, and they work me over with words of praise and sweet, sweet degradation.

"Such a beautiful whore," Pierce groans. He leans down and sucks one of my nipples into his mouth harshly, coming off of it with a loud pop.

"So filled for us, and still a greedy slut," River says in my ear before biting down on it and pinching my clit.

I moan around Phoenix's dick, and he fists my hair. Hard. "Come for us like the cumslut you are, Red. Then swallow us all."

My eyes roll to the back of my head as I come for them, stiffening in their arms and barely hanging onto reality as they each come inside of me. I swallow Phoenix's cum like the good girl he wants me to be, and he rewards me with a kiss as Pierce and River squash me in a sweaty heap between them.

I love being the meat in this sandwich.

I grin, lazy yet exhilarated, and hum when they pepper kisses along my skin.

River and Pierce pull out of me, then Phoenix pulls me from the bed and carries me to the bathroom, where he starts a bath and pours my bubble bath into it.

Strawberry soda drifts around the room, and I sigh.

Content.

Happy.

Home.

I frown a bit at that, but ignore it in favor of leaning against Phoenix in the bath and closing my eyes.

"Can we stay here forever?" I ask with a yawn.

His hands drift up my body, washing away the sweat from the day and the exhaustion from the last few weeks.

He's done this every day since I've been home, and it's perfect. With every bath, the feel of abusive touch goes away, and I sleep better than the night before.

"If this is where you want to plant your roots, Red, we'll do it." Phoenix presses a firm kiss to my temple and begins massaging my scalp until I'm putty in his arms. "You're the queen around here. We do what you want."

"Hmm." I peek up at him through my lashes and smile when he does. "Then this is home. For all of us."

He kisses the tip of my nose and nods. "I love you."

Too lazy to talk, I lift my hands and sign *I love you, too.*

# phoenix

The concept of home is unique for each of us, it seems, because for the last three days we've all taken up different tasks around the house.

Pierce has ignored all responsibility so he can work on the fence and yard.

River has dedicated most of his time to redecorate as much as he can. Rae scolds him constantly, making him put all of her mother's old pictures back up and sends him to the basement.

That's officially the man-cave, she says. We can change whatever we want about it, but the rest of the house needs to stay as close to the same as possible, or she'll murder us all.

Or worse, deny us sex.

Since we can't have that, River has redone the entire basement, adding our pool table from the loft, and organizing the gaming systems.

It looks kind of sweet down there, but it's still not a priority.

I've spent the last few days making sure everyone eats and taking care of the laundry. I've always done these things, but it seems like, with a house and nothing else to do with our time, it gets messier faster. And no one pays as much attention to what's happening around them.

Pierce and River could never really just be kids. Never allowed to just exist.

So now they're stuck. They don't know what else to do.

"He's got a sunburn," Rae says as she hops onto the counter. She yanks the spoon from the brownie batter I was mixing and sticks it into her mouth.

"I wasn't done with that," I playfully snap. I tap her thigh, then shake my head and place my hands on either side of her on the counter. Leaning in, I keep my eyes on hers as I pull the spoon into my mouth and lick the rest of the batter off of it, leaving it empty of the treat she wanted so badly.

"Rude," she says. She rolls her eyes and tries to dip the spoon back in, but I grab her wrist to stop her.

"That's disgusting."

"Nix, you and the guys literally share me all the time. Spit. Cum. Sweat." She yanks her hand free and grabs a heaping spoonful of batter, then stuffs it into her mouth. "This is fine."

A line of chocolate drips down her chin and I lean in to lick it up, then kiss her. Our tongues tangle together and I revel in her sweet whimpers.

"Something's beeping!" River shouts as he enters the kitchen. "Oh, hey, I didn't realize it was make-out o'clock!"

Rae giggles as she leans back to stare at him.

He kisses her firmly, then points to the oven and stares at me.

I glare, but remove myself from between Rae's sweet thighs. I take the brownie batter bowl and pour it into the pan, then place them inside the oven. After setting the timer, I lean against the counter and look out at the yard. "He's done well with it."

"We sound so domesticated and shit," River says. He hops up on the counter next to Rae and sticks his finger in the mixing bowl before stuffing it into his mouth.

"I don't know who you think 'we' are, River, but you are far from domesticated. Should keep you outside on a leash." I grin when Rae chuckles and runs a hand through my hair.

"There's only nine days left," Rae says sadly, reminding us we're being watched.

Constantly.

And Maxwell Langston *will* come for her.

"Plan is still the same, RaeRae." River tosses his arm over her shoulders and pulls her to his side. "We even have confirmation that the rest of the crew is meeting up in the right place at the right time."

She nods and chews on her lip as she watches Pierce out of the window.

We all know the biggest flaw in our plan is that someone has to keep them inside until the bomb goes off.

And Pierce has already stated, clearly and more than once, he's going to be the one to do it.

"It'll work out," I tell her. Though I don't trust the entire thing yet.

"Hey," River says, hopping down off the counter. "Let's go for a drive. You and Pierce can tell us stories, and we can work on planning our future here, yeah?"

She shrugs, but the tiny smile stretching her lips calms my nerves a bit.

The elephant in the room refuses to be ignored for the next nine days, but we're still going to try.

After River grabs Pierce from the backyard, we all hop into the Jeep with the top down and the wind blowing against our heated skin.

Summer is trying to beat down on us early.

"Fuck," Pierce breathes as he turns onto Main Street. "Half of these buildings are still run-down as fuck. Do you think Hargraves will pay for those to be fixed, too?"

"Looks like he already is," I say, pointing toward a large construction crew lingering outside of the supermarket. I grin at the memory of Rae and me coming here for food around Thanksgiving, and kiss her cheek when her eyes meet mine. "Guess it's getting an upgrade."

"Feels like we're all starting fresh," she says. She intertwines her fingers with mine and looks at the other side of the street. "Five years from now, this will be such a different town."

"It's needed it, though," Pierce says. "Half the time, we'd play inside the buildings, not knowing if we'd get shot or get a disease from a rusty nail."

Rae snorts at that.

"So," River says, turning back to study Rae. "What does our future look like here, RaeRae? Tell us, so we can make it happen."

Her entire face lights up with the dreams in her head. "I want to help other girls. Abuse survivors."

"There won't be abusive fucks in this town if I have anything to say about it," Pierce snaps.

"There's always some dickhead, though," I tell him. I shrug when he glares at me in the mirror. "Better to offer self-defense classes and a shelter."

"I want to do that," Rae says. "Open and run a shelter."

Pierce nods, and points at a large building surrounded by grass. "The old community center work?"

"It would need another floor, but yeah." She sighs and leans her head against my shoulder. "It's too much money, though."

"Well," River says, "once my parents die, I'll get a hefty sum from life insurance."

"I've got a ton of money left, too." My parents had the best damn insurance after my brother started getting sick, and life insurance came with it. Family was priceless to me, but the money lasted a long ass time.

Besides, my grandfather still insists on sending me fucking money monthly.

"We've also got that one guy. We could pull a Robin Hood. Steal from the rich, give to the poor." Pierce grins.

"What will you guys do for work? We can't all just stay at the house all the time." Rae looks around at us when we stare at her. "What? I cannot deal with all three of you twenty-four seven!"

"I'm hurt, RaeRae," River says, holding his hand over his heart.

"Shut the fuck up," Pierce snaps. He laughs when River smacks the back of his head, and points toward another building further down the street, not even a block from the community center. "Says that building is for sale. Wasn't that Old Pete's Garage?"

He pulls into the driveway and stares for a moment before turning to the rest of us with a raised brow.

"This was our dream for Junk, right?" I ask. We'd talked about setting up a garage after college, extensively. Now was as good a time as any, especially with a large FOR SALE sign sitting out front. I pull my phone out of my pocket to check the details out online.

"Riv?" Pierce turns to him.

River nods a few times, then grins and claps his hands together once. "Hell fucking yeah! Let's do it."

Rae smiles and settles back against the seat. "Three hot, sweaty mechanics and a woman with a vengeance. Sounds like the start to a good porno."

"What the fuck do you know about pornos, sweet girl?" River asks.

"Don't ask," Pierce and Rae say at the same time. Their eyes meet and they break out into laughter, reminding River and me that there will be many things we know nothing about between these two.

"It's bought," I tell the guys, pocketing my phone. "I also put in a request with Hargraves for the community center."

"Wait," Pierce says, turning to me with a question in his eyes. "Really? Like... this is ours?"

"It's ours."

"Well, shit," he breathes. He straightens in his seat and we all stare at the run-down old building, while our future in it flashes before our eyes.

We drive around for a few more hours, taking in all the renovations and the things that are staying the same. It's like this guy came in and took out all the awful shit in one full sweep.

By the time dinner rolls around, Rae begs Pierce to pull into an old diner, and we plaster our asses to the sticky vinyl seats while we wait.

"Well, I'll be damned," a woman drawls, her warm green eyes tracing over every feature of Raven's face. She does the same to Pierce and pats his cheek. "I never thought I'd see you two back in this town again. What the hell are y'all doing back?"

Rae snuggles into Pierce's side and smiles brightly. "We wanted to come home, Mary. That's all."

"Oh, my lanta. When did you get your voice back?" The woman places the coffeepot down and reaches over to grab Rae's hands.

"Not too long ago. Still hurts sometimes, but the more I use it, the better it is." Rae grins when Mary kisses her forehead.

"I'm so glad, sweetheart. So, so glad. I'm gonna order y'all a pizza, then get you some chocolate pie. On the house, alright?"

"Oh, you don't—" Pierce says, but she waves him off.

"Nonsense. I'm so damn glad y'all are home." She turns on her heel and walks back to the kitchen, yelling out our food order as she goes.

"Well, she's nice," River says, smiling.

"Pretty sure she's shipped us since the fourth grade," Rae says. She chuckles when Pierce rolls his eyes. "I used to bring him here all the time when I knew his mom hadn't fed him."

"And I'd yell and complain the whole time, even though I knew I'd leave with Miss Mary's leftovers so I could eat a few days after." Pierce sighs, but smiles as he looks out the window.

"Man, I hope she picks on our kids as much as she's picking on you two."

All eyes snap toward River, and his face pales.

"What? What did I say?"

"Kids?" Rae squeaks, then clears her throat.

"D-Do you not want kids? We don't have to. I mean, it would be nice but—"

"River," I sigh, placing my hand on his shoulder, "you're thinking way, way too far into the future right now."

"Let's get through the Maxwell bullshit first," Pierce says. He looks over at Rae and they share a silent conversation.

She shakes her head, then looks out the window with a distant look in her eyes.

## *raven*

Kids?

I didn't think I'd survive half the shit the guys put me through back at CU, and now we're talking about *kids*?

I squeeze Pierce's hand as we walk back up the driveway, urging him to the side of the house.

He knows where I want to go.

We walk through the field in silence. Past the trees. Into the abandoned playground.

"Looks like Hargraves hasn't found this yet," Pierce says, coming to a stop near the edge of the wood-chipped area.

"Is there a way we can buy the property back here?" I pull him toward the swings and release his hand once I sit in my usual spot. It groans with my weight, and a few flakes of rust fall to my feet, but I still swing a little.

Pierce's hands cover mine on the chains and he pulls them back before releasing them and taking a small step back. He presses firmly on the small of my back each time I swing toward him, and it calms me to know we can still be like this.

Quiet.

Contemplative.

Together.

"I'll have Phoenix do the adult thing and reach out."

I giggle at that. "Poor Nix. He's the only one having to really adult around here."

"Pretty sure he wouldn't have it any other way, babe." He sits on the swing next to me and rests his head against the chains, watching my swing slow.

Our eyes meet, and I smile for him, but my heart hurts because my father is still out there. Watching. Waiting.

Less than nine days.

"Hey," Pierce says, lifting my chin with his fingers. "What happened just now?"

"One of us has to keep them in that basement," I whisper.

"Yeah, and we've been over this. I'll be the only one in and out of there. It'll be quick."

"Lance and Mark both said it'll go off too fast after you set it." Tears escape my eyes and I swipe them away angrily. "There's gotta be another way to do this."

"The government doesn't care, Rae." He huffs and stands, stuffing his hands into his pockets as he paces in front of me. "No one fucking cares. I'm sure there's a million other ways to do this, but this is the plan. This is what we're doing."

I stand and shove his chest, more pissed now because I'm angry crying and I hate angry crying. "You're gonna die!" I screech.

"So fucking what?" he roars back at me.

I take a few steps back and gape at him.

"So fucking what if I die, Raven? Life's been pretty fucking miserable except for when I've been with you, and if keeping you from him means I have to die, then I will. To save you," he says, grabbing my wrists and pulling me into him, "I'll die a thousand times."

"I can't live without you," I whisper.

"Yes, you can. You have Phoenix and River. They'll love you better than I ever can, and you know that."

I growl as I slap him across the face, wincing as my palm stings and I see the angry red mark on his cheek. "You've loved me our whole lives, Pierce Jackson, and you promised me you'd love me forever."

"And this is me keeping that promise."

"No," I snap, shaking my head. "If you aren't with me forever, you aren't fulfilling your promise. Because," I hiccup when my cries grow harder, "because forever would suck without you."

He sighs and runs his hands through his hair, then reaches forward and grabs me, pulling me into him and holding me in a tight hug.

Warmth envelops me, but I still feel so cold at the thought that he's going to die.

"I can only promise to try my best to get out of there fast, babe, but I can't promise anything else."

"You've been walking around looking like you're already going to die, Green." I look up at him and rest my chin on his chest as our eyes meet. Both of our eyes fill with tears. "Promise me you'll try everything to live."

His lips crash down on mine, and he kisses me for a long time under the moonlight in our special place.

But he never promises.

I sigh and hold his hand tight as we walk back toward the house where River and Phoenix wait for us.

"I can't believe River brought up kids," Pierce says. He chuckles and shakes his head.

"The world is too scary for kids right now."

"Agreed. But," he says, pulling us both to a stop, "what if this town really did turn out better? What if what Hargraves is doing gives us a safe place to raise them? What then?"

I chew my lip as I stare down at my feet.

"Rae?"

"I guess, if everything is good, and they'd be safe, then I'd love to get back to our dream of having a house full."

He grins and kisses my forehead. "I guess the guys and I have a shit ton of work to do on the house. We'll need tons more space."

"Tons?" I squeak. "How many are you thinking?"

"At least a dozen."

"Pierce Jackson!" I yell as he takes off running, laughing. "I will not have a dozen fucking kids! I want to do other shit with my life!" I stumble into the kitchen, nearly knocking Nix over as he tries to catch the door from smashing me in the face.

Pierce jumps over the couch and lands beside River, using him as a shield. "She's gone feral!"

"Listen here!" I point at all of them and plant my hands on my hips. "If we have kids, I will settle for three. One from each of you. After that, I'm done. I want to do something else with my life outside of laying down and spreading my legs for you!"

"Uh." Phoenix folds his arms over his chest and raises a brow. "What the hell is going on?"

"Nothing. The matter is settled." I huff and sit down in

the recliner. I grab the remote from River's frozen hand and switch on The Notebook.

If they want me to suffer, I'll do the same right back to them.

"Pup," River drawls. "What the hell did you do?"

"Mentioned that maybe we should have a dozen kids." Pierce says innocently.

"Absolutely fucking not!" Phoenix snaps, coming over to smack Pierce upside the head.

River barks out a boisterous laugh and shakes his head. "Let's get through the rest of this year first, yeah?"

I curl up in the recliner and pull a blanket over myself, smiling when Pierce and River snuggle up together.

We need to enjoy just being us first.

And get through my father's bullshit.

Alive.

# CHAPTER NINETEEN

## *pierce*

Rae whimpers, and I pull her body tighter into me as her body trembles.

I'm so fucking sick of her nightmares. Not because I'm tired of taking care of her, but because I'm tired of the assholes who caused them.

"Shh," I whisper in her ear. "It's okay, little bird. You're safe."

She whimpers again, and I kiss her forehead.

I tuck her hair behind her ear and kiss the top of it, but before I can whisper anything else to soothe her, a twig snaps outside and I shoot straight up out of bed, sending River crashing to the floor.

"What the hell, pup?" he groans as he rolls onto his back and stares up at me with tired eyes.

"Watch Rae," I whisper. I glance back to check that she's still asleep, and when she rolls over to curl into Nix, I breathe a sigh of relief. Grabbing a pair of sweats, I slide them on and ignore River's whispered questions as I grab a gun from the top of the dresser and peek into the hallway.

The wood on the back steps creaks as I tiptoe into the hallway.

"What the hell is going on, Pierce?" River whispers harshly as he follows behind me.

"Shut the fuck up," I snap. "Someone's outside."

"Man, it could be Julian or—"

The backdoor opens, so I hold my hand up to tell River to shut it and step slowly down the stairs.

The wood is cold beneath my feet, but my body is hot as the blood rushes through my veins, roaring like an inferno, ready to burn everyone in my path.

A set of boots appear around the corner just before a man in all black does, and I raise the gun to his head immediately.

Fucking Jimmy Perkins.

"Hands up, motherfucker," I spit as I hit the final stair, glaring at him as he faces the barrel of my gun.

He stutters, but when I press the end to his forehead, he shuts right the fuck up. As he should.

"Basement, River," I order, shoving Jimmy's shoulder so he moves.

If Rae sees he's managed to sneak in here, her nightmares will get worse.

"I-I-I—"

"Shut the hell up, Jimmy." I shove him again and grin as he stumbles. After I've closed us into the darkness, I follow them. Before he can make it to the last stair, I swipe my foot out and kick him in the back of his knees, sending him tumbling down the last half-dozen steps.

The crunching and groaning make me happier than I've ever been.

Almost.

"Tie him the fuck up," I tell River, ignoring the glare I get. He can punish me later.

"Listen, guys," Jimmy says, "I came here to—"

"Do I look like I give a flying fuck what you came here to do?" I snarl. I punch him in the nose and smile when blood spills and bone breaks.

I've been waiting years for this.

River finds a folding chair and some rope, and we work together to tie Jimmy to it.

Then, because I'm feeling feisty, I kick it over so his head bounces off the concrete below it.

"Fuuuck," he groans.

"You've been a pain in my ass since I was eight years old, Jimmy. That's a little over a decade. I've barely had the chance to beat your ass the way I've wanted to without getting arrested." I chuckle and pick up a hammer off a box from when River and I were hanging shit earlier. "But here you fucking are, barging in on my goddamn home, trying to get to my goddamn girl. Again."

Jimmy squeals when I lift the hammer, and just like his little frat buddy, pisses himself just as I come into contact with his knee.

Well, we only teased his frat buddy.

This time, I smash Jimmy's kneecaps in with the hammer and groan when he breaks.

"You assaulted my girl over, and over, and over." I punch him in the side, then lift the chair up and stare him directly in the eyes. "I have plans for you, motherfucker."

"Wait," River says, "like... those plans?"

I grin wickedly at him and nod. "Those plans."

"Hell yes!" River bounds up the stairs, and I roll my eyes.

If Rae wasn't awake before, she will be now.

"Keep quiet while we wait for him to bring your present down here, Perkins." I lean back against the wall and tap the hammer lightly against my arm. "You're in for weeks and weeks and weeks of torture, my friend."

His eyes widen, and he shakes his head as he protests behind the tape.

I ignore him.

"Alright. What size are we going with?" River asks as he bounds back downstairs with a box in his hands.

A box full of pineapples.

Jimmy looks curious, but by the time River and I take out a few, he looks rightfully terrified.

He knows what's up.

"So, Jim-boy," River sing-songs. "It's about time you knew what it was like to be violated, yeah?"

"You see, we're a house full of assholes, sure, but we all know what it's like to be abused in one way or another. Unfortunately for you, you abused our girl in a way only River knows." I shrug and help River untie Jimmy, and we begin stripping him.

It's disgusting and enraging to imagine this fucker laid out over my girl, using her body in the way only we should be allowed to.

Pretty sure I should chop his dick off, too.

But that'll wait.

"I must have forgot the lube upstairs," River says with a fake pout.

I laugh. "Oh no. That's just rude."

He shrugs and Jimmy continues to squeal as we tie his hands behind his back and shove him to the ground.

I plant my foot on the back of his head to hold him

down, then look over at River and wave toward his ass. "Go for it."

"I'm gonna burn my hands after this." He wrinkles his nose, but he still bends down and lets out a maniacal laugh as he shoves the pineapple up Jimmy's ass.

His screams are glorious. Not even the sight of his blood all over the basement floor deters me from enjoying them.

"Now Jimmy," I say with a sigh, "it sucks when someone takes something from you, huh? When they fuck your body up so bad you can't think?" I reach out and grab his head, forcing him to nod. "Thought you'd agree."

"Pierce?" Rae whispers.

I whip around and stare at her, wide-eyed.

"Wh-Jimmy?" She backs up, running into Phoenix, who keeps her steady as her knees buckle. "He got in?"

"For the last time," I tell her. Because he's dying tonight. Right fucking here. I sigh and glare at Jimmy again. "See what you did? You woke her up." I punch his side again and grin as he falls over, screaming in pain as the pineapple no doubt continues to torture his insides.

"You guys are disgusting," Phoenix says as he tries to pull Rae back up the stairs. "This is too much."

"It's not enough," I snap. "It will never be enough to make up for what he's done to her!"

I turn back to Jimmy and kick his stomach. Over and over and over again until he's puking on the floor, crying out, and his screams are the only sounds I hear.

"Pierce," River says, pulling me back after who knows how long. "Come on, that's... it's enough."

"No," I snap, turning to glare at him through the angry tears in my eyes. When the fuck did I become this emotional? "It's not."

"You're scaring her," Phoenix says. He's holding Rae against his chest, her eyes on a half-lifeless Jimmy.

She's crying.

Why the fuck is she crying?

"Rae... baby... I..." I sigh and thrust my now bloodied fingers through my hair. "Wh-what did you want me to do? He deserves more than this." I gesture to him on the ground.

"I'm gonna take her upstairs. She's in shock." Nix shakes his head as he turns her. "Clean this shit up."

"No," Raven says quietly. "No," she says again, this time more firm.

"What?" Nix asks, brows furrowing in confusion.

"I... want to finish this."

"Red, you don't—"

She shakes her head to stop his protests. Turning, she walks over to where I placed the gun and picks it up. Her hands tremble.

I should probably stop her before someone else gets hurt, but I don't.

We all watch, transfixed, as she moves to where Jimmy's head is.

He's crying out behind the duct tape, tears and snot falling in streams down his face.

"I should let them draw this out, you know?" she says. "But no one ever gave me mercy, and I'd like to think I'm better than the rest of you." She lifts the shaking gun and presses it to the center of his forehead, much like I did not too long ago. "Giving you mercy will bring me peace." Then she pulls the trigger, and the shot rings out in the basement for so long, I wonder if the sound will ever leave.

No one says anything as we watch her deal with this.

She stares and stares and stares at Jimmy. The guy who

abused her and manipulated her for so long, I'm surprised she ever stayed after I attempted the same shit.

"Rae," I whisper, and that's when she collapses backwards. I catch her, lift her in my arms, and carry her right past the other two.

They'll clean this mess up while I take care of her.

"Shh," I whisper in her ear as she cries and cries.

She cries through the shower I make us both take.

She cries in the bath that I draw her to help soothe her.

She sobs in my arms on the bed as I hold her close to my chest, wrapping us both in the blankets.

By the time she finally stops crying, Phoenix and River climb into bed, freshly showered.

We soothe her to sleep.

While I know Jimmy's death ends the torture...

The nightmares will never end.

She gave him the mercy no one ever gave her.

And that's why I love her.

# raven

It's been two days since I shot Jimmy Perkins point blank, and I still can't get his look of terror out of my head.

Nor can I get rid of the vision of Pierce repeatedly kicking a naked, bloodied man in the stomach.

He was shouting. Practically foaming at the mouth.

And yet, here I am, curled up in his lap on the couch for comfort, watching The Princess Bride while River massages my feet and Phoenix strums a guitar out on the porch.

We're relaxed.

We're young.

But we're still not free.

Pierce's phone beeps and he kisses my forehead as he leans forward to grab it off the coffee table. As he reads the message, I keep my eyes locked on his, searching for worry or panic. Instead, his eyes light up and he smiles. "Well, little bird, it seems Grayson Hargraves is willing to sign over the community center to you."

I sit up in his lap and crack a genuine smile. "Really?"

He nods and shows me the message. "Yep. Says he wants to meet up at the beginning of June to discuss building plans."

"That's three weeks from now! We need to draw up plans!" I rush to the front door and open it, peeking my head out to look at Nix. "We got the center! But I need plans. Like... today!"

"Three weeks!" Pierce calls.

"Today!" I reiterate to a confused Nix.

He picks his guitar up and carries it inside, kissing my cheek as he passes. After he places it in the case, carefully, lest it get a smidge of dirt on it, he looks at me expectantly.

"Hargraves is letting me have the center. He wants me to meet up with him at the beginning of June with the building plans. Please help me draw them up like... as soon as possible."

"Let me write up a business plan for it first. We'll discuss the building plans later." He wraps me up in a hug and rests his chin on my head. "Did he say how much?"

"Free of charge, if he likes our plans." Pierce stands and stretches. "I need to call Lance. See what's going on back at Junk and the school."

"Julian get the security hooked up?" Phoenix asks, and I pull away to go sit back down on the couch next to River.

"They got to talking about adult stuff again, huh?" he chuckles, pulling my head onto his lap so he can massage my scalp.

"Yup." I sigh and close my eyes. "I'm tired of adulting."

"I like certain parts of adulting," he says, sliding a hand down to cup my ass.

"River," I scold, giggling when he slaps my ass.

"Fine. I'll be good." He yawns and gets more comfortable

on the couch with me, and before I know it, we're both fast asleep.

"I DON'T KNOW why the fuck he'd be calling," River snaps. He stands and sets my head on the cushion gently, before stomping his way out of the room.

"Well, if you'd answer the phone, it wouldn't go off twenty times in an hour!" Pierce shouts, following him.

"The hell's going on?" I ask. I sit up and stretch, looking at Nix where he sits in the recliner, his guitar on his lap.

He works to restring it, brows furrowed in concentration. "River's dad has been calling him repeatedly for the last hour. He won't pick up, and the buzzing annoyed Pierce. So now they're bickering." He waves his hand in the direction they took off.

"Why would River's dad call?" As far as I know, River's dad hardly called him at all. Ever since the would-be engagement party at the cabin, no one has contacted us outside of the message Maxwell sent Mark to give us back at Junk barely a week ago.

Should have known that wouldn't last long.

River bounds down the stairs, grabs a beer from the fridge, cracks it open, and downs half of it before staring out at the backyard.

"What happened?" I ask Pierce as soon as he steps into the living room.

"His dad said he was coming to the school next weekend."

"But that's when—"

"We're meeting up with Maxwell? Yeah." Pierce sighs and sits back down on the couch next to me. "Seems our plan is working."

"Who else confirmed?" Phoenix asks.

"Lance said everyone. Maxwell, Priscilla, Robert, Melissa, Mark, Whittaker, Adelaide..." Pierce takes a deep breath and looks down at his feet. "My mom."

"Six days left." I curl my knees up to my chest and rest my chin on them as I watch Nix work the strings on his guitar.

"It'll be fine," Pierce says, looking pointedly at River. "I keep telling him this, but he's still worried."

"We're all worried about you, because you're going to be the only one going in there!" River tosses his beer into the trash and folds his arms. "You're gonna get killed."

"That's what I keep telling him!" I point to River and glance at Pierce. "He agrees with me. You're doing the dumbest shit and it's gonna get you killed."

"I'm tired of this argument," Pierce snaps. He stands and walks out of the room, leaving River and me fuming, and Nix sighing and shaking his head.

"Wanna help me punish the pup for his attitude, RaeRae?"

I look at River and raise a brow in question.

"C'mon," he says, waving his hand in front of me for me to take.

I take it and stand up, letting him lead me upstairs and into the main bedroom.

Pierce lays flat on his back, arms behind his head, as he stares blankly at the ceiling. He barely moves his gaze to us before rolling his eyes. "What now?"

"I think you need a little attitude adjustment, pup."

River leads me to the end of the bed. He lets go of my hand and crawls over Pierce until the two are nose to nose. "You're not acting like a good boy."

"Riv—"

"Nah," River says, placing his hand over Pierce's mouth. "You've done enough talking. The words you're using are rude and not at all the ones you should use when speaking to those you care about."

Pierce narrows his eyes, and River moves his hand down to his throat, collaring it as he sits on Pierce's torso.

They stare at each other for a few seconds, and I watch, transfixed, as the chemistry between them sizzles and crackles and roars to a flame.

I clench my thighs around nothing and bite my lip.

"Hey, little vixen?" River asks, not moving from his spot on top of an immovable Pierce.

"Hmm?"

"Be a good girl and grab the rope out of the bedside table."

Fucking hell. I love the dominant River. He may not act like it, but he knows how to control everyone in a room.

I do as I'm told, grabbing the lube for good measure, then crawl onto the bed and sit cross-legged next to them as I hold the items out to River.

"Thanks," he says with a quick kiss to my cheek.

"River, I'm—" Pierce tries to say, but River squeezes his throat.

"Going to keep your mouth shut before I gag you." River rips Pierce's shirt off and uses the rope to tie Pierce's hands together before securing them to the hook on top of the headboard.

"When...?" I ask, looking around the bed for any other hidden spots.

"We had to do something with our free time when we couldn't be out there looking for you, little vixen. We created most of these with you in mind." River winks at me as he slides down the bed, pulling Pierce's pants and underwear down with him. He tosses those to the side and works on securing his ankles to posts at the end of the bed.

Sprawled out and helpless, Pierce's jaw tightens as he glares at River, his cheeks pink in embarrassment.

"Don't be shy around RaeRae, pup. She's seen all of you."

"Not like this," Pierce grumbles.

"Because you hide," River states simply. He leans over the bed and kisses Pierce's stomach, ignoring his hard dick, which is begging to be touched.

I lick my lips as I sit there, watching them, waiting for whatever my part in this is going to be.

River walks to the closet and pulls out a large chest, opens it, and pulls out what looks like a whip, but with many long leather strands on the end. "Ask me to punish you, pup. Ask me to punish you while she watches. After that, I'll let her sit on your face and you can make her come as an apology."

That's it. They're going to kill me. Death by horniness.

"P-Please," Pierce stutters.

"Please, what?" River asks as he saunters back toward the bed. "I'm going to flog you no matter what. It's whether I make it good or bad for you that's determined by how you use your words, pup."

Pierce growls in frustration, tightening his hands on the rope and glaring at River.

River raises a brow and cracks the flogger down onto Pierce's thigh, forcing a yelp out of him, followed by a groan.

His dick twitches, and a bead of pre-cum leaks from his tip.

I lick my lips.

"Don't touch, little vixen," River warns. "Not yet."

I fist the sheets beside me and nod my head, watching as he trails the toy up and down Pierce's side.

The way his muscles flex and contract... is mesmerizing.

River hits him again, this time on the chest, and Pierce groans. "You haven't asked for it yet, pup. I could leave you tied up here for an hour. Take her, please her myself. Come back later and make you take a cold shower."

"You wouldn't fucking—OW!"

River gets him in each pec this time, leaving behind tiny little welts that I'm deeply inclined to lean over and kiss better.

"Please," Pierce pants, staring pleadingly at River. "Please punish me while she watches."

"And then?" River asks, leaning over the bed and getting back in Pierce's face.

"And then can I please make Rae come as an apology?" Pierce grits through his teeth, his eyes flashing over to me for a split second before going back to River.

River pats Pierce on the face a little hard, then stands back up and slides the flogger down his body, smacking it a few times, but not enough to mark him. "Count like a good pup," he says right before swinging the toy and connecting with Pierce's thigh.

His back arches and he groans. "One."

River cocks a grin and hits him on the other thigh, below his hip.

"T-Two," Pierce pants.

I'm so wet right now. I'd place bets on me coming solely from this.

River again taunts Pierce, sliding the flogger all over his hips, his waistline, his dick. He meets my eyes and hits Pierce again, this time on his stomach, right above his dick.

"Motherfucker, that was too close!" Pierce shouts. He's panting, sweating, and his dick looks like it physically hurts.

Glad to see I'm not the only one being tortured.

"That didn't sound like a number," River sing-songs, lifting the flogger again.

"Three!" Pierce growls at him.

"Say it nicely, and I'll let it count." River grins, waving the toy in the air.

"Three," Pierce says, calmly this time.

"See," River says cheerfully, "you can learn how to be a good boy." He hits Pierce's ribcage twice in quick succession.

"Four," Pierce says between deep breaths. "Five."

"Good boy," River praises. He tosses the toy onto the bedside table and comes around to the side of the bed I'm sitting on. He pulls me into an embrace and slides his fingers down, down, down, until he can plunge them into my underwear. "Damn," he groans in my ear, plunging his fingers into my wet cunt. "She's so fucking wet, pup. Did you like that, little vixen?"

I swallow as I train my eyes on Pierce's heavy-lidded stare. "Yes."

"Here, pup," River says, pulling his fingers out of me. He leans over the bed and stuffs them into Pierce's mouth. "Taste how much you turned her on."

Pierce groans around River's fingers, sucking them deep into his mouth and cleaning them.

River pulls away and helps to strip me, then lifts me onto the bed. "Sit on his face and let him apologize."

I don't hesitate. I climb all the way up and grip the headboard as I hover right over Pierce's face.

River sits on the bed beside us and unties Pierce's hands. "You only use these hands for good, pup, or I tie them back up. Understand?"

Pierce says nothing. He grabs hold of my ass and pulls me down directly onto his waiting mouth. His tongue explores and takes as the stubble from his chin rubs against my thighs, fueling sensation after sensation.

"Oh my god," I whimper as my thighs shake.

"Put your entire weight on him, little vixen," River coaches from beside us. He's stroking his own cock as he watches us, and I tighten my thighs around Pierce's head. "He'd be happy to suffocate by your sweet little pussy."

"You're filthy," I whisper. Pierce digs his fingers into my ass tighter and swirls his tongue around my clit, forcing a moan out of me.

"Scream for us when you come, little vixen."

I lean my head against the headboard and groan.

Pierce pushes me up enough to stuff his fingers deep inside of me, curling them against my g-spot. "Soak my face. Fly for me, little bird." His eyes lock on mine intensely as he leans back in and sucks my clit between his lips.

My thighs shake and my heart stops beating. My head falls back on my shoulders and I scream, the sound echoing around the walls.

Pierce groans as he continues to work me over, and I feel it as he comes, the stickiness hitting my back when River does the same.

They soak me like I do Pierce's face, and I lose all sense of myself as my chest heaves and my heart pounds.

After a few minutes, Pierce lifts me and works with River to settle me on the bed between them, their arms wrapped over me as they hold each other's hand. They watch each other for a beat, then River kisses him, then me, and yawns.

"You're exhausting as hell," he complains, closing his eyes.

"I'm sorry," Pierce says, kissing the top of my head. "One day I'll be able to stop being such a dick."

"Yeah, that'll be when Hell freezes over," River says.

I snort and bury my face against River's chest.

I'll never admit it to anyone, but I wouldn't change Pierce Jackson one bit.

His temper tantrums always end up with me being rewarded, after all.

# river

"It won't fucking budge," Pierce grumbles for the hundredth time.

"Yank it harder," I snicker.

He glares and kicks the fence, yelping when it gives, and he nearly goes tumbling to the ground after it.

I grab his arm to steady him and laugh. "One of these days, you'll have to stop throwing tantrums. They're gonna get you hurt."

His cheeks turn bright red, probably remembering what we did yesterday, and he turns to pick the last piece of fencing up from the ground.

It doesn't take much longer before we've got the yard cleaned up and we're setting up the new fencing around the property.

The property Pierce extended with a small little chat to Hargraves.

Pierce and Rae's abandoned playground now resides on our property, which extends half a mile into the woods.

It's romantic as fuck, and I adore being part of their love story.

"Hey," I call to him an hour later. "Grab Nixy boy and let's take our girl on a picnic."

He pauses and raises a brow at me. "Really? What are we, five?"

"Nah. There's only four of us."

He chuckles before he can stop himself and walks back into the house to do as he's told.

Shocker.

I pull my phone out of my pocket and silence the call from my father. Again. Before all this shit went down, I'd be lucky to get a call from him once a month. Now, unfortunately, it's multiple times in an hour.

He wants me to meet up with him and mom when they come to do a campus tour.

Little does he know, I'm one of the tour guides, and they won't be leaving.

Pain slices through my chest when I imagine the look on their faces as we lock them in the science building... with a bomb. They don't deserve my grief, but they'll probably get it anyway.

The thing about narcissists is that, if they're good at it like my parents are, you'll still be sad when they leave.

"Jeez, it's hot," Rae says as soon as she bounds down the back steps.

"Summer's trying to make an early entrance," I say as I reach for her hand and tug her into the trees. "Means your birthday's coming up soon, huh?"

"July fourth." She looks back at Pierce. "His is the fifth."

"I know. I have all sorts of dirty things planned for the two of you."

Her cheeks color, and she shakes her head. "Filthy, River."

I shrug.

Ten minutes later, we're all sitting in the safety of a weeping willow that Rae led us into, and Nix is handing out sandwiches.

"Do you think Maxwell can see us out here?" Rae asks.

"If he can, I have a feeling he gets more impatient by the day." Pierce takes a bite of his sandwich and leans against one of the tree branches.

"Five days left," Rae whispers. She picks at her sandwich for so long, I worry she won't eat at all, but after humming to herself, she sits up straight and dives right in.

One of the reasons I love her is because she loves to eat.

Even if she does hate coffee.

"I'm getting impatient waiting for the day we take him down," Pierce grumbles around his food.

Nix rolls his eyes. "We all are, but without knowing where the hell they all are, it's easier to get them to meet in one location at the same time."

"I just want to start living my damn life," Pierce snaps.

"Are we not already living it?" Rae asks, worry in her tone.

"I mean... we are," Pierce says, "but—"

"If you aren't happy with the way things are right now, let's fix it." Rae sits up on her knees and glares at him. "What needs to change, huh?"

"Well, nothing, but—"

"Then stop fucking complaining. Yeah, it feels like the world will topple at any damn moment, Pierce, but at the end of the day I get to curl up between all of you. Then, in the morning, I get to wake up to all of you." She sits back down and leans her head on Nix's shoulder. "That's good enough for me."

No one speaks for a while, and the heat finds its way into our small den of safety, forcing us to pack up and head back to the house in search of cool air.

It's all so... mundane.

Easy.

"You know," I say to Pierce as we pack up back in the kitchen, "we could get a head start on cleaning up that garage. If you want."

He stares blankly out the window for a moment before sighing. "Yeah. Let's go."

We leave the house, kissing Rae on the cheek as we pass, and hop on the bikes Lance and his crew brought down this morning.

"Fuck, it's good to be on this baby again." I groan when my bike fires up and smile as I put my helmet visor down.

Pierce takes off like a bat out of Hell on his Ninja, and I follow. He never slows, though, and while the lack of police presence worries me, it seems to not worry him at all.

We wind through alleyways, down what seems like every street, and take the scenic route around town. Minutes turn to hours as we wind through the hills surrounding Aurora Falls, and I get the feeling he's blowing off steam. Appropriately, this time.

He pulls into the parking lot next to the old garage, the SOLD sign right in front of the building telling the world there's a new owner in town.

Unsure if he plans to sit on his bike for the rest of eternity, I take off my helmet and run my hands through my hair. I need a haircut. "Hey, Pierce." He looks over his shoulder at me, brows furrowed. "We gonna go in or...?"

He nods and turns off his bike, then climbs off and pulls the keys out. The door creaks as he opens it, and he has to rattle the knob half a dozen times before it'll release the key. "This is going to be a lot of work."

"It'll keep us distracted for these last few days, at least." I stand shoulder to shoulder with him inside the main lobby of the old garage. Butterflies take flight in my stomach as I imagine what it could be like.

"I didn't think I had a future, much less one with her in it," he mumbles, as if he's afraid to disturb whatever's in the air right now.

I wrap my arm around his shoulders and pull him in. "Yet here we are, pup. This is ours. We just gotta work our asses off to make it successful."

"I should write down what to do in case I'm not here to fix it up with you." He makes his way into the office, and I follow.

"You aren't going to become a martyr, Pierce."

"I'm just preparing."

"No need. You aren't dying. Besides," I scoff, "I'm going down with you so I can drag your sorry ass back to our girl."

"Bullshit!" he snaps, standing to his full height and slamming his hands onto the desk. "I refuse to risk you, too."

"Then you aren't risking me, or you." I kiss his lips to shut up the rest of his protests. I lean back and gesture around the room. "Let's get to work, yeah?"

# raven

Two days.

That's how long we have left until we go back to Cobalt University under the guise of hosting a campus tour for Maxwell and all those who worked with him.

Every single action they took in the past affects us now. While I've never seen myself killing anyone, it seems it's the only way to take these assholes out.

"Get on the bike, baby," Pierce says a little too sweetly.

I may be skeptical of his actions, seeing as the last time he let me drive a bike, he screamed at me for three hours.

"Please?" he asks. He shows me the puppy dog eyes I'm sure he's used to giving River, but I roll my eyes at him.

I still get on the bike, though.

Covered head to toe in leather, complete with the red jacket the guys gave me for Christmas, I'm sweating. From the heat and the nerves.

"Now, you have to put your hand here and pull," he

instructs, showing me exactly what to do with my hands. "Keeping your balance will be a bit hard on the turns, so just take it up the street and stop. One of us will come and help you turn it around."

"You know, I would have learned better back at Junk had you treated me this nicely then."

He rolls his eyes and plops the helmet down on my head. After clipping it in place, he grabs the helmet with both hands and places a kiss on the helmet over my forehead. "Be careful, okay? Take it slow."

"Yeah, yeah. I hear you." I place my hand on the handlebars, lift my feet, pull, and jolt forward too fast. With my heart in my throat, I stop the bike again entirely and panic when I can't keep it standing.

Phoenix rushes toward me and holds the bike up. He looks over at Pierce and raises a brow. "You needed to tell her to pull it slow." He looks back at me. "Slow, Red. Understand?"

I nod, and when he lets go of me and the bike, I slowly pull the throttle. Crawling down the street on the bike seems ridiculous, but it's the best I've got on my second day.

The last one shouldn't count, but Pierce insists it does.

"Yeah!" River shouts as I pass him halfway down the street.

I grin behind my helmet as I make it to the end and stop the bike again.

Pierce's bike roars in my ears as he makes his way toward me. He comes to a stop beside me and helps maneuver my bike around so I'm facing the cul-de-sac, then pats me on the ass and watches as I take off again.

This time, I try to turn so I can go again, but the bike wobbles, tips, and I go flying with it.

Thank god for protective gear, or my body would scratch to all hell and I'd probably sprain something.

I lay on my back, splay my arms and legs out and groan. But I smile.

Because adrenaline is still my favorite drug.

"You see why I didn't let you do this last summer?" Pierce asks as he helps me stand. He lifts the helmet off my head and grips my chin in one hand, tilting it this way and that until he's satisfied I'm safe.

Butterflies swarm when he leans in and kisses me.

"Bike's good but scratched," River calls from a few feet away.

With a grunt, Pierce moves away and grabs my hand, tugging me toward his bike. He doesn't have to tell me what he wants, so when he climbs on and passes my helmet back to me, I happily put it back on and climb on behind him.

"Be back soon!" he yells to the guys, then takes off down the street with a laugh.

My heart hammers in my chest and my cheeks hurt from smiling as he drives us through streets, past the community center and garage, and out toward the coast.

This was our favorite pastime last summer, and as the happy memories flood my thoughts, I close my eyes and allow myself to simply exist.

Pierce removes one of his hands from the handlebars and slides it up my thigh, squeezing gently as he leans back a little. "Remember this moment forever, Blue!"

I open my eyes and meet his through the tiny mirror above his handlebar.

His are filled with sadness and determination, and it hurts.

He really thinks he's going to die.

I squeeze my arms around him tighter, only to release him a few seconds later and spread my arms like I used to do.

To pretend I'm flying.

I yell into the sky, and he does too as he takes us around the mountaintop. The water of the coast is on our left, shimmering in the afternoon sunlight.

Fuck, it feels good to be this free.

A few minutes later, Pierce pulls into the parking lot next to an old hiking trail, parks, and turns off the bike. He lifts the helmet from his head, shaking his sweaty hair free before tapping my thigh.

"Come on," he says, voice a little rough from yelling.

I hop off and remove my helmet, placing it on the other handlebar and grinning when he reaches forward to fix my hair.

He tucks it behind my ear and stares for what seems like forever before kissing my forehead and reaching for my hand.

We walk in silence for a while, hands swinging between us like we haven't a care in the world.

Two more days. After that, we won't have to worry so much anymore.

"I never thought we'd be back here," I whisper.

He glances down at me for a second, then helps me over a fallen log and leads me down the path. "Pretty sure the last time we were here, it was what? Not even a week after your mom found out we boned for the first time?"

Scoffing, I smack his shoulder and shake my head. "Who says 'boned' anymore? And yeah, she found out and immediately questioned every single time we were alone in my room, or yours, or at the park." I giggle and grip his hand tighter as we walk the last few feet to our destination. "She thought we'd been screwing around our whole lives, and I had to yell to get her to shut up long enough to listen to me."

"We totally should have been screwing around that long."

I roll my eyes. "You were the one who was too much of a pansy to date me!"

"Didn't want to break your heart. That's all."

"You ended up doing that, anyway."

He sighs and releases my hand so he can push the brush away.

The waterfall roars as it pours into the clear pool at the bottom. Not a soul knows this exists but for Pierce and I. At least that's what we told ourselves when we found it years ago.

I sigh and smile as I walk toward it.

"Rae," Pierce says quietly, turning me by the arm and meeting my eyes. "I'm still so fucking sorry."

I shrug.

"No. Please listen." He lifts my chin with his fingers and stares intently at me. "Everything I've done since September has been extremely shitty."

"Not everything," I interrupt.

"Most of it," he amends. "I don't know what I did to deserve your forgiveness, but I plan to spend forever apologizing."

My smile grows until my cheeks hurt.

"What?" he asks, brows furrowing in confusion.

"You said you plan to spend forever apologizing."

"Yeah, I know what I said. What about it?" He tilts his head to the side as he studies my happy expression.

"You don't plan to die tomorrow."

He rolls his eyes and pulls me in until his chin rests on my head and he's got me wrapped up in his arms. "You're obnoxious. I've only been making plans, just in case."

"There is no other option." I say for what feels like the thousandth time. "You won't die. You can't."

"But what if—"

"Nope."

I'm gonna stay in Denialville for as long as possible and he can suck it up.

"Impossible woman," he grumbles but lets me go.

We both watch each other hungrily as we strip to our underwear, but it's not enough for me. Not this time. I pull my panties and bra off and toss them with our clothes, then turn and take a running leap into the pool.

"RAVEN!" echoes around us.

I cackle, and screech because *holy shit, the water is fucking cold.* When I resurface, Pierce is standing there naked as the day he was born, his half-hard cock stealing my attention.

"Keep staring, see what happens."

"That's the type of threat I can get behind." I place my finger on my chin as I pretend to think. "Or in front of. Beside. On top—"

"Alright, alright," he laughs. He takes a running jump and splashes into the water directly in front of me, sending water cascading over my body, forcing me to take a deep breath. He grabs me and pulls me into him, encouraging my legs to wrap around his waist as we resurface. "You're turning into a dirty little whore, Raven." He shakes his head as if he's disappointed.

I snicker and kiss the ball of his shoulder, then rest my chin on it and look around us at the forest hiding us from view.

Hiding us from our problems.

"We should bring the guys out here," Pierce rumbles in my ear. He kisses my neck softly, exploring with his tongue. Taking his time to enjoy me.

"We should." I expose more of my neck to him and allow him to take it.

All I've ever wanted was for him to take everything I've ever offered him.

"I never in my wildest dreams thought I'd be okay with sharing you the way I do, Blue." Threading his fingers through my hair, he tugs my head back so he can stare into my eyes.

I grin lazily. "And yet, I also share *you*, Green."

His cheeks turn red with his blush, and he narrows his eyes when I giggle. "He centers me."

"He disciplines you. Something no one's ever done properly."

Snorting, he kisses my nose and releases my hair to slide his hand down my back instead. He palms my ass and wiggles his brows. "Didn't know Dick Discipline was a thing."

I bust out laughing and thread my fingers in his hair.

"It wasn't that funny," he says when I keep laughing.

"It," I snort, "totally fucking," I gasp, "was."

"Seems you might need some Dick Discipline." His brow arches and he reaches between us to tease my clit, lighting a roaring fire in my veins that quickly kills my laughter.

"Pierce," I breathe.

"I missed your voice, little bird," he says.

"I missed it, too," I confess, arching my back as he continues working his magic. "It was so hard some days.

Especially when you guys would get busy and weren't looking."

"I'm sorry we weren't always looking, baby." He leans in and kisses me, prying my lips apart to apologize with his tongue in my mouth.

Logically, I know they couldn't always watch me to see what I had to say, but the emotional parts of me struggled.

I squirm as he slides a finger inside of me slowly, moaning into his mouth. Sharing my pleasure. My desire. My chest rises and falls rapidly as he adds another finger and pumps inside of me lazily, putting pressure on my clit with the heel of his palm. With his hand on my lower back, he forces me closer to him, even as he pulls his mouth away from mine to watch me.

"Come for me," he says quietly as he applies more pressure and pumps his fingers faster. Harder.

Watching him watch me and work me over so intently sends me into a slow, quiet, but powerful orgasm, and my head nearly falls under the water as I gasp out my pleasure.

He doesn't waste time between my orgasm and shoving his dick inside of me. He removes his fingers, spreads my legs, and thrusts inside. Exactly where he belongs. Groans of pleasure rumble through his chest and into my ear as he begins kissing my neck again. One hand holds my ass, guiding it in the rhythm he fucks me in, and the other threads in my hair again, holding me close and still.

He makes love to me.

Worships me.

And when we both come together, crying out into a loving kiss, it reminds me how much I love this man.

How much I've always loved this man.

We wade through the water like that for a long while, his dick still inside of me as we hold each other, existing in the same moment and reveling in the calm before the storm.

"I love you, Raven."

"I love you, too, Pierce."

# phoenix

"Goddamnit, Raven!" Pierce shouts.

Putting me on fucking edge.

Again.

I place my guitar back in the case and stand up, about ready to beat the hell out of his disrespectful ass.

Rae giggles.

My heart calms, and I smile.

I knew well before she got her voice back that she could handle herself, but not hearing her do so made it hard to stay in one place while she put Pierce in his.

Still doesn't mean it's any less stressful hearing him be an asshole.

"Don't do it," Pierce warns.

Fuck it. Their drama entertains me.

I step into the garage and lean against the doorframe, folding my arms and taking in the scene in front of me.

Rae has a can of spray paint in her hand and is aiming it at his bike, where a streak of vibrant purple already shines on the side. Her eyes flick to me and she gives me a once over. She waves the can in the air before looking back at Pierce with a devious smirk.

"Do not fucking do it, Raven Marie," Pierce snaps.

River chuckles from his spot next to his own bike.

Pierce glares at him. "Stop encouraging her!"

"Oh no," River deadpans, fighting to hold back laughter. "I can't believe she'd add a little color to your life. It's awful. I'm so sorry."

I laugh, hard, drawing all of their eyes to me.

Raven snorts and turns to spray Pierce on the back instead, the paint staining his white t-shirt. She tosses the can and books it toward me, sneaking underneath my arm and hiding behind my back.

"Why would you think I'd save you from that, Red?" I ask as I stare at her over my shoulder.

She shrugs and tries to sign something, no doubt to keep Pierce from seeing, but he rushes toward us.

I block the doorway and hold firm when he tries to shove me.

"Get out of my way, Nix," Pierce growls.

"Say please."

He huffs and glares at me.

"Wait," Raven says, slapping the back of my shoulder.

I look back at her. "What?"

"You'd give me up just like that?" she screeches.

"I mean," I shrug, "bad girls do get punished."

Her cheeks flush a gorgeous shade of red, almost as vibrant as her hair. "But—"

"Gotcha!" River says, lifting her from behind. He must have snuck around and in through the front door.

"River!" she squeals and laughs when he tickles her.

Their penchant for acting like children used to annoy me, but recently it's just been nice to be part of it.

I lean toward her and grab one of her bare feet, and tickle it while Pierce does the same to her other foot.

She thrashes, squeals, cackles, cries for help.

"What should we do with our little brat?" River asks, grunting when her elbow connects with his stomach.

I'm about to suggest something far more fun than tickling her to death, but I'm interrupted by the doorbell.

"Lance is here," Pierce says. He kisses Raven on the forehead and walks toward the front door, the purple standing out drastically on his back.

Pain sears through my shoulder when Raven punches it and I glare at her. "Really?"

"You were gonna give me up with some half-assed apology from the grumpy one!" She scoffs and turns toward the door.

"Well, hitting isn't a good girl thing to do either," I mutter in her ear. "So your punishment just got worse." Goosebumps rise on her skin as I place a kiss behind her ear.

"Damnit, Nix." She shivers and crosses her arms over her chest as she walks into the living room after Pierce and Lance.

"I can't believe this shit," Pierce snaps. He's pacing the living room in front of the coffee table while Lance sits on the recliner, elbows on his knees and hands clasped together.

Our eyes meet for a split second before he looks back at the ground.

"What happened?" Rae asks in a whisper.

"I... we were coming back to Junk—"

"Why'd you even leave?" Pierce asks, voice full of bitterness.

"We were putting safeguards in place for the meeting." Lance grits through his teeth.

Pierce sighs and Raven steps over to him to wrap her arm around his waist in a hug. He rests his chin on her head and waits for Lance to continue.

"They burned what they could, but when that wasn't enough," Lance winces, "they blew it up."

Everyone turns to watch Pierce, expecting yet another tantrum.

But he laughs.

He laughs hard.

And when Raven meets my eyes, I shrug.

"The beautiful fucking irony," Pierce says before kissing Raven's hair.

"Okay then," Lance says. He lets out a long breath. "That leads me to point number two. We're going to move the team into Aurora Falls. Actually," he says, "we've already started. There was a house for sale across the street and—"

Raven bursts into laughter.

My lips twitch, and I fight my laughter as I shake my head. I glance over at a very confused Lance. "Need help with anything?"

He shakes his head, still watching the other two lose their minds. "No. We've got enough guys moving shit around."

"Let's go out back," I say, turning and walking toward the backdoor.

Lance steps outside with me. He rests his forearms on the porch railing, while his eyes drift across the backyard and the new fence. "Damn."

I sit down on a step and rest my elbows on my knees and take a deep breath. "Have we—"

"There's no getting him out of there," he interrupts.

"What do they have on him? Have we found that out?"

He shakes his head. "We had someone working on it, but he recently went dark."

"He okay?" If anything happened to anyone on his team, regardless if we knew them personally, I'd feel like shit. Especially if it gets tied back to us.

"I hope so. But they locked the files down. Maybe once Langston and all the other fuckwits are gone, we can search for them. But Phoenix," he says, sighing, "don't get your hopes up, okay?"

I shrug and study the ground. "Everything Lexi's father touched ended up ruined. Her brother was MIA before we even got together. Her mother is either strung out or too brainwashed. Lexi is—"

"Dead," Lance says.

"Right." I sigh. "It's all absurd. I couldn't imagine pleading guilty to something I didn't do."

"Are you sure he didn't?"

I lick my lips before meeting his gaze. "A thousand percent positive. He was willing to kill anyone for her. Anyone. You could see it in his eyes."

"If he's capable of murder, why wouldn't he kill her?"

"When I visited him before spring break, he was strung out. He had given up, but not because he did it. No," I scoff. "They want him in there because he never suited their way of thinking. I'd have been in the same position if I had stayed with her."

Lance takes a seat on the stair next to me. "Whittaker is one of these fucks, right?"

I nod.

"Then tomorrow will be the end of it."

I don't argue with him or point out that grief never ends. Standing, I turn around and make my way back inside.

If there's anything I need right now to ease this stress, it's my girl.

"We'll be right behind you tomorrow," Lance says. He pats my shoulder and waves at Raven and Pierce on the couch.

As he closes the door, I turn toward them and fold my arms over my chest. "You two sane again?"

*Define sane,* Raven signs after shoving a chip in her mouth.

"Hey, what's for dinner?" River calls as he comes back inside from the garage.

"I was thinking Raven," I say, turning toward him and grinning.

"Thanksgiving part four?" River shouts. He claps his hands together and grins at the other two.

"Thanksgiving part four sounds great." I turn around and make my way back into the kitchen.

If my role in our little family is to put smiles on their faces with delicious food, I'm more than happy to take it on.

"WHERE DO you think you're going?"

Raven turns around slowly and shrugs. She looks like she's in trouble.

She's not wrong.

I'm going to punish and fuck away every bad thought she has about tomorrow.

And the guys are gonna help me do it.

"Come here." I pat my thigh while keeping my gaze pinned on hers.

Pierce and River sit back in their chairs, more than willing to watch the beginning of this show. I half expect River to strip immediately, but he sits in his chair and watches with hungry eyes as Raven walks across the dining room.

We may have just eaten, but dessert is only beginning.

"We have a lot to get ready for tomorrow." Her eyes drop to the floor. And I hate that.

"Look at me," I command.

She does.

"I already told you what I want to do." I fix a strand of her hair before threading my fingers in it and tugging enough to keep her eyes on me. "Do you want us to fuck the racing thoughts away, Red?"

She licks her lips and swallows, then nods as best she can with the tight hold I have of her.

"Then sit your pretty ass on my lap like a good girl." I release her hair and pat my thigh again. Waiting.

She goes to straddle me, but I turn her around and yank her shorts and underwear down her legs. I pull her down on my lap, coax her legs over mine, and yank her back to my front.

"Nix," she stutters, jerking slightly when I pull her head back onto my shoulder.

"You're our little toy. No thoughts, Red."

She squirms in my lap, the cool air no doubt creating its own sensation over her newly exposed skin.

"Do you understand, Raven?" I ask her when she doesn't respond.

"Yes," she breathes.

"Good girl," I praise. I love praising her almost as much as I love fucking her. "Now," I whisper in her ear, "let's give the boys a show until they're aching for you as much as I am."

Without hesitation, I stuff two of my fingers inside her already soaking pussy.

# raven

I've never felt so wanton in my entire life. It's like Phoenix could *hear* the thoughts running around in my head during dinner. As if they all knew I was thinking the worst of tomorrow and now they seek to fuck these thoughts out of my head.

Just the look in Phoenix's eyes after I turned back toward him made me wet. But when he demanded I let him fuck the thoughts out of my head?

Yeah. It's embarrassing how soaked my underwear became in such a short amount of time.

"You're still thinking," he rumbles in my ear. His fingers pump inside of me slowly, like he has all the time in the world.

We don't.

"Take your shirt off, Red." He stops moving his fingers, but doesn't remove them as he waits for me to do as I'm told.

I swallow harshly as I remove my shirt and bra, tossing

both to the floor next to my other discarded clothes. Embarrassment doesn't even cross my mind as I sit on display for all three of my men, waiting for them to devour me with more than just their eyes.

Phoenix maneuvers my legs back over his thighs and spreads his legs, opening me up for River and Pierce to see. Pleasure zings through me as he pumps his fingers again, grinding his hard dick against my ass as I squirm and seek more.

Always more.

"You're so wet for us, Red." To prove his point, Phoenix pulls his fingers away and stuffs them in my mouth, forcing me to taste myself. He tugs a little until my mouth opens wide and a long string of drool falls to the floor beneath us. "Making a mess already, baby?" He groans and kisses my neck. "Get on the floor and crawl to them."

"Jesus," Pierce mutters, adjusting his dick in his pants as River does the same beside him.

"Gotta say Nixy boy," River chimes in, "your dirty talk might make me fall in love with you, too."

Phoenix snorts and closes his legs so I can get on the ground and do as I'm told. "Make them come for you, Red. Like a good girl."

The cold floor barely penetrates my senses as I lock my eyes on River and Pierce and begin crawling to them like the good little slut they've turned me into. Maybe I was always this way, and they just let me open the door to this side of me. Everything that's happened has to have happened for a reason, right?

And if that reason is so that I end up on my hands and knees, crawling toward the men who hold my heart?

Fuck it. I'd do it all over again.

My ass stings before I realize what's happened. I turn around in shock and see Phoenix's brow raised and his arms crossed over his chest.

"Stop thinking," he commands.

I turn back around to the other two and lick my lips at the sight of them pulling their dicks out. Just for me.

"Stand up," Phoenix says. I look at him, confused, but he points at the other two.

They don't question him. They stand up when I make it to the floor in front of them and sit back on my haunches.

I peer up to see the gorgeous sight that is Pierce and River, staring at me with love and lust in their eyes as their cocks stand proud. My hands reach out of their own volition and I stroke, eliciting twin groans from my men. I don't hesitate for a second before reaching out and licking the beads of pre-cum leaking from them both and allowing the salty taste to mix with my desire on my tongue.

It's filthy and beautiful.

Exactly how we should be at all times.

"Gorgeous little vixen," River whispers, almost as if he's in awe.

I take him into the back of my throat, eyes locked on his, then swallow him down a little further, squeezing him as I do Pierce with my hand. They moan in unison, and I squeeze my thighs together, seeking a reward Phoenix won't allow me too soon. So I work them over, alternating between them and getting more turned on by the mess I'm making of us all.

Pulling so they come close together, I keep my eyes locked on their faces as I move my mouth over both of their cocks, stretching my lips wide. I can't take them too far back, but I make up for it by stroking them with my hands and swirling my tongue around their heads.

Watching them tremble.

Fall apart.

Shake.

"Fuck," Pierce grits through his teeth. He looks over at River, who simply nods before they both stuff their hands inside of my hair and pull until my head tilts back and I'm staring up at the ceiling.

River groans just before they both come on my lips, chin, neck. Down my chest.

It goes everywhere.

Before I can move, River shoves Pierce to his knees. "Clean her up," he commands. He leans down and kisses me with such passion, I don't know where I end and he begins. His tongue duels for dominance as Pierce licks the mess from my body, letting his hands trail along my skin and dig into places I wish he'd keep them.

I groan and wiggle. Place my hands in their hair and pull, trying to gain some control. The needy, slutty part of my brain seeks release.

"Come here, Red," Phoenix says, voice penetrating the haze River and Pierce have left me in.

I glance around until I can see him, and he crooks his finger from his spot on his chair again.

He's naked.

Waiting.

Looking at me like a starved animal and I'm his dinner.

Yes, please.

I crawl to him, and his lips quirk into a sadistic grin as he watches me. At his feet, I pause and peer up at him through my lashes. Waiting.

"Climb up here, Red, and see what happens to good girls."

Happily, I oblige, moaning when the first thing he does is impale me on his dick, slamming up until our hips connect and my swollen clit gets the attention it's seeking.

"Did you like your mouth full of two cocks, Red?" he asks. He leans down and bites one of my nipples. He holds me still, fighting off my need to squirm with a bruising grip.

"Yes," I moan breathlessly.

"Good girl," he praises. His eyes lock on mine and he moves my hips, grinding me on him at a tortuously slow pace. "Ride me and make us both come."

I nod frantically and do as I'm told again, grinding myself on him and holding onto his shoulders. My nails dig into his skin as I frantically seek release.

He rolls his hips under me, and his piercing reaches new angles I never thought possible. Another bite to the nipple. Another pull of my hair. A hickey or three on my neck.

I don't know what's happening anymore.

All I know is I want more.

River and Pierce step toward us, and each of them takes one of my nipples into their mouths. They suck, bite, play. They watch.

Phoenix tosses his head back on a groan, squeezing my hips and pushing me down further on his lap.

The friction sends sparks through my body that escalate to full on fireworks when Pierce reaches down and pinches my clit between his fingers.

I scream and Phoenix comes a few seconds later, holding me on his dick as I grind and twitch.

Pierce and River leave kisses along my skin, then

matching hickeys on either side of my neck. They pull away with their own praises and whispered sweet nothings.

My entire body shakes for so long. I don't know what the hell to think, except that a bath with Phoenix sounds nice.

And a glass full of cold water might be a good idea.

# maxwell

Today is the day my daughter officially returns herself to me and her mother.

The day my son takes her, and they share my last name for the first time.

Some may say that having my children marry is disgusting, but I want a pure bloodline, and this is the best way to keep it.

It's all biblical, really.

Sommers and Jacobs would be proud.

"Maxwell, darling, would you help me with these wretched lapels?"

Taking a deep breath, I turn around and grin at my wife.

Together since middle school, all throughout high school and college, we've survived a lot together. Yet the only woman on my mind constantly is Chloe Jackson.

She stole my heart before Priscilla got pregnant, and the day I found out I was going to have a child, I had to man up and end things.

Of course, many years later, I found out she'd been with

someone else during our time together and had a child of her own. I was furious, but really had no grounds to be. Still, I took revenge on her by using her and her son to gain access to my daughter.

If only I could get my hands on my sister Everlyn. Pull her from the grave and kill her all over again. It wasn't enough to poison her by way of Chloe. I wanted to have a direct hand in her death, just as I did her fuckwit of a husband, David.

"Maxwell?" Priscilla calls, pressing her hand to my cheek.

I look down into her blue eyes and wish I felt the same love I did for her back then. It was magical. *Was.* "Sorry, dear wife," I mutter. I reach out and help her with the lapels of her business jacket, straightening them to within an inch of their life.

"She's coming back to us today," she says. Statement, not a question.

"Absolutely. After that, she'll take our name and we'll finally be a family." I kiss her forehead, imagining Chloe's instead. "Just like you've always wanted."

It doesn't take long to get the rest of us ready, and while we sit in the back of our town car, Chloe on one side of me and Priscilla on the other, I try to call Jimmy again.

It's been days since I've heard from him, and I'm growing more concerned by the day.

Chloe clenches her fingers together, then unclenches them. Over and over she does this movement until I reach out and grab her hands, stopping her.

Our eyes meet, and the fluttering in my heart reminds me of who it belongs to.

"It will be okay. Pierce will come around, Chloe."

She shrugs and pulls her hands away from mine, giving a pointed look in my wife's direction.

My wife, who was told no less than a dozen times that she'd have to deal with Chloe being on my arm from now on.

I can't live the lies I was before.

Not now.

Not after everything we've been through.

"He wants me dead at this point, Max." She shakes her head and looks out the window.

"He's too much of a coward to kill anyone." I'd be dead by now otherwise.

Sighing, she sits straighter and works on composing herself for the rest of our drive to Cobalt University.

Where it all started.

And where it will continue for generations to come. Generations with my name in big bold letters. I already drew up the papers to buy the school. I only need this pesky shut down to end and the FBI to stay off my ass.

Getting Walter Starling fired was the first step.

Unfortunately, Pierce Jackson and his fucking crew, along with my ex-best friend Mark Riley, thwarted all efforts to get the campus addicted to Rapture.

For now.

I have more plans.

More labs.

Step two is gaining access to the main labs in the science building again. That being shut down has caused more havoc than Pierce could ever try to create.

"Does she hate us?" Priscilla asks me as we enter through the gates to find their Jeep parked in front of the admin building.

I throw my arm over her shoulder and pull her close to me, then kiss her head. "No. She doesn't hate us. She just needs to get to know us better."

"She didn't try when we had her for two weeks, darling."

"Jimmy will set her right." I check my messages from him again, unread and unanswered. "I'm sure he will."

"Sir," my driver pipes up as he slows near my parking spot.

"You can stay in the car for now, Gerald," I tell him with a pat to his shoulder. Looking over at Chloe, I gesture toward the door. "Open it. Let's set things right."

She inhales deeply, closes her eyes, then exhales as if the world is about to crush her.

I won't let it.

Priscilla gets out, then Chloe finds her strength and opens her door to get out as well.

I grip her hand and hold it tightly as we climb out side-by-side. With the split second we have before our children notice us, I kiss her cheek and lean close to her ear. "I promised I'd fix it all for you, love," I whisper, then pull back and release her hand to fix my suit jacket and wrap my arm around my wife.

"Langston," Pierce greets warmly.

It gives me pause.

"Jackson." I nod, then look toward his side where my daughter stands and smile for her. "I'm glad you've come to your senses, dear daughter. Are you all staying for this tour as well? I've heard there was a benefactor looking to renovate some things and wanted to speak with me."

Phoenix West steps forward and holds out his hand. "That would be me. I still have money from my family's unfortunate end and wanted to spend it on the school that's allowed me to find family again."

I raise a brow, but accept his hand and shake it firmly. "I'm glad we've allowed you to find family here, Mr. West."

He nods and pulls back to stand next to Pierce and River. They stand as a united front, as if I didn't already view them as such. Jacobs would be proud of his son, standing in unison with his frat brothers.

I still have no idea where Jimmy is, but once I take my daughter home, we'll put out a search party if we have to.

"So, what were the plans for the school, gentlemen?"

A couple of cars pull up in the parking lot. I furrow my brows in confusion. I had no idea anyone else was coming to tour the campus today.

The first person to step out grins when she sees me, her white hair up in the tight bun it's always been in since we were teenagers.

"Well, if it isn't Adelaide Winfield," I call out to her. The moment she's within reach, I pull her in for a hug. While she became closer to Jacobs after college, we'd been friends since freshman year and she was paramount in helping me set up the business side of things.

"Oh, Maxwell," she says, pulling back. "It's been too long."

"It has. It very much has." I shift my gaze to another car, watching as Whittaker and his wife step out. A black SUV reveals Robert Jacobs and his wife. A beat-down white car reveals Jimmy's mother, the bane of my goddamn existence.

"What the hell is she doing here?" Priscilla snaps from my side.

"It's not like I invited her." I pat her arm gently and wait for the crowd to come join us. "You're all here for the tour?"

Whittaker grins and steps forward before wrapping me into a side hug. "We heard someone was going to help rebuild. Make this place better than ever."

"And foot the whole bill," Robert says, shaking my hand.

We share greetings with the women before turning toward the crew of kids who called us in.

"Our first order of business is the science building," Phoenix says, gesturing us in that direction.

"What are your plans for it?" I ask him. I allow my wife to walk behind me and closer to our daughter, who hasn't looked our way once. She'll learn to love us as soon as she's away from these boys.

"A few things," Phoenix says.

"Wait," Whittaker calls out before catching up with us. "This heathen is going to foot the bill to fix the school? Unlikely. He never had dreams outside of his little garage band."

"Well, Mr. Sommers," he starts, "your daughter is the reason I have this money. And since you loved to encourage her, I suppose you could thank her for the money."

"Nix," Pierce says, elbowing his side.

Whittaker scoffs and shakes his head, but says nothing more.

Robert looks at his son, standing as close as possible to Pierce, and narrows his eyes before scowling and shaking his head.

"I'd say it's a great thing these boys want to help, brothers." I step in front of everyone and walk backward so I can see them all. With arms wide open, I smile. "It's a new era. Alpha Mu will be restored. The school will have better facilities. These boys know giving back is the best way to go in life." I point toward Phoenix. "You'll go far, especially with your fellow Alpha Mu Alumni behind you."

He grins and nods, but says nothing as we continue.

I turn back around just as we hit the stairs to the building, then furrow my brows when Pierce heads toward the basement door. "What's happening?" I ask with a slight chuckle.

"We really wanted to upgrade the lab first," he says, looking toward Phoenix, who nods once. Shoving open the basement door, Pierce gestures down it. "Don't worry, the lights are already on. We needed one more benefactor for this particular project and they've got the blueprints down there and ready for review."

"Very... thorough of you, Mr. Jackson." I make my way down the staircase, the others at my back, and something niggles at the back of my brain. Like this is a trap.

Surely it isn't, though.

Couldn't be.

These kids are too young and dumb to set me up at all.

With that thought in my head, I grin and adjust my suit jacket and take the final step into the basement.

Well-lit and clean as can be, it seems nothing is out of place from the last time I was in here, determined to produce Rapture at a fast enough rate to get every student addicted and lining my pockets. Until I notice a man sitting on a stool in front of a lab table. A man I haven't seen since he snuck into my house and nearly gave me a heart attack weeks ago.

"Mark Riley," I spit, gritting my teeth. "I told you what would happen if I ever saw you again, didn't I?"

"Oh, you did," he says, a little too cheerily. As if his death is something to be celebrated.

"You have some—"
*Bang.*

# *pierce*

I slam the door closed as hard as I possibly can, grinning when the women downstairs squeal and the men turn around to glare at me as I descend the stairs. With my arms crossed over my chest, I shrug and make my way closer to Riley. I have the final piece of his little puzzle, and I'm the one who has to start the timer when I'm done saying what I need to say.

"Apologies folks," I lie. "The door wouldn't close normal. Had to give it a bit more force. Something I imagine we can foot the bill for when we rebuild this place."

Maxwell narrows his eyes at me. "Why is Mark Riley working on the blueprints for this building?"

"I'm not," the man in question says. He smiles his stupid crooked smile when Maxwell turns to glare at him. "I'm simply here for the fireworks."

"What are you even—" Maxwell tries to ask, but I interrupt.

"At what point did you think kidnapping Raven was a good idea? Before or after she moved in with us last year?"

"Excuse me?" he snaps, glaring at me.

I move further into the room.

Closer to Riley.

Closer to the bomb sitting behind him inside of the lab table sink.

"I'm simply asking at what point you knew you were going to take away all of her rights. Oh, wait!" I snap my fingers. "We got the recipe, and you knew it! So it had to be after Thanksgiving." Grinning, I lean against the table and shove my hands in my pockets, feeling for the timer. I grip it in my hand and tilt my head as I watch Maxwell seething with anger and stuttering in confusion.

"If you had kept your hands off her, Jackson," he spits, taking a step toward me, "she wouldn't have stayed with you. She would have easily come with Jimmy. Or come to me when your self-righteous bullying became too much for her."

"See, Langston, I've never been too much for her." I grin when his face turns a scary shade of purple. "In fact, I was never enough for her. Hence the extra guys to satisfy her every need."

"Pierce Jackson!" my birth-giver and life-sucker snaps.

I turn toward her. "I'm sorry. I don't listen to narcissistic assholes anymore."

"I don't understand what's going on here," Robert Jacobs says, stepping forward and looking at Riley. "What are we all doing here?"

"I thought this was a tour of the campus..." Whittaker Sommers says.

"I mean, it is a tour. Your last tour." I turn around and press my forearms on the counter, acting as if I need a moment. I place the timer firmly where Riley showed me with trembling fingers, and press the button to start the two-minute countdown.

Not long enough, Raven had argued.

Too long, I'd yelled back at her, regretting it immediately. Like I always do when I do anything to take the smile from her face.

Riley's eyes bore into me as I slowly pull back and turn around. He tries to nudge me with his foot, but I walk toward the center of the room.

In the middle of the crowd of shitty humans and even shittier parents.

"Each one of you had a hand in the way this turned out."

"Pierce," my mother snaps again. "This is absolutely ridiculous and completely overdramatic."

I bark out a laugh. "Overdramatic, mother? Really?" Shaking my head, I open my arms toward them all. "This entire thing was overdramatic before I was fucking born. You." I point toward Maxwell. "You set up a drug-trafficking ring on a college campus, including an entire fraternity that you built for that purpose."

He tries to speak, but I hold up my hand to stop him before he gets any more bullshit out.

"You," I say to Robert and Whittaker. "You both steal young kids and fuck them or fuck them over. Either way, you ruin their lives forever. I'm surprised River can love–and fuck–as good as he can after everything you've done to him." I direct the last bit toward Robert. "The rest of you are just complicit in their bullshit. You're either too drugged up to care," I say, glaring at River's mother. "Or too damn busy chasing the next big thing," I say, staring blankly at mine. "Some of you are ignoring the entire situation and going about life as if it's perfect and you're the best wife and mother ever." I look between Maxwell and Whittaker's wives and shake my head.

"Why am I complicit?" Jimmy's mother squeaks.

I'd forgotten she was here, honestly.

"You gave birth to and raised a human almost as shitty as Maxwell." I snort. "Oh, and he's dead, by the way. Raven killed him."

Gasps and curses roll around the room, but I'm not listening anymore. They mean nothing to me. Absolutely nothing.

Turning back toward Riley, I nod my head back toward the door, but he shakes his. I frown. Yes, he helped the entire thing happen back then, but he's the only one who has reformed himself. He suffered enough.

Death isn't for those who have learned to apologize and mean it.

"It seems to me," Maxwell says, clapping a hand on my shoulder, "that you've locked yourself in the lion's den, son."

"Do. Not. Call. Me. Son." I spit, ripping his hand off me. Before he can react, I punch him as hard as I possibly can in the side of his head.

"TEN!" Riley shouts, and my gut churns as Maxwell tries to swing back at me.

"Ten what?" Whittaker asks.

I don't need to be told that I'm running out of time.

With the promise of not dying I made to Rae and the guys, I attempt to book it up the stairs.

Maxwell grabs my ankle and I go sprawling down them, my face impacting the corner of at least five. "You're not getting out of here without getting taught a very valuable fucking lesson, Jackson."

"Eight!" Riley shouts, panicked.

I have to say goodbye to Rae from here, I guess.

"Seven!"

"What the hell is going on? Did you plant something?" Maxwell spits in my face as he spins me on my back. He grins, and the blood pouring from his nose gives me a sick sense of satisfaction.

"Six. Jackson, get the fuck out of here!" Riley shouts, then grunts.

"What did you do?" Maxwell growls at me.

"What we all should have done twenty years ago," my mother says, a coldness in her voice I've never heard before.

"Five!" Riley shouts again.

I close my eyes and welcome death.

A loud pop forces my eyes back open just in time to see my mother holding a freshly fired gun directly at Maxwell's temple, blood spewing from his head.

"Mom...?"

"Four!"

I look up the stairs, then back at my mother, heart slamming hard in my chest.

"Go, baby. This is what we deserve," she says, tears trailing down her face, "but it's never been what you deserve."

"Mom, I—"

"Three!"

"GO!" she screeches.

Blinking back my own tears, I push Maxwell's dead body off me, turn, and scramble up the stairs.

Riley doesn't need to shout the last two numbers. As soon as I exit the basement, close the door, and attempt to book it far enough away to not catch major bodily harm, the bomb explodes and sends me flying halfway across the courtyard.

"Pierce!" Raven and the guys yell.

The building collapses. I think. The brick crumbling is loud enough to penetrate the ringing in my ears.

My body slams hard into the ground, and my head bounces.

"Oh, my god!" Raven screeches.

I grin and open my eyes, barely seeing her pretty blues before having to close mine again.

"Pierce, man," Phoenix calls, slapping the side of my face.

I grunt.

"Pup," River yells next to my face.

I smile.

"Green," Raven sobs, pulling my head into her lap.

I open my eyes one last time and smile. "I freed you, little bird. I freed us all."

Her tears are the last thing I see before the world falls into blackness.

# raven

A FEW WEEKS LATER...

"Ready for this, RaeRae?" River asks for the trillionth time.

He's more nervous than I am.

"Yeah," I whisper. I take a deep breath before adjusting my bun for the twentieth time.

Okay, so maybe I'm a little nervous, too.

"Let's go!" Phoenix calls from downstairs.

"No." I shake my head. "Not ready. Can we like... go back a few days? I'm totally not prep—"

"Chillax," he croons, wrapping me up in his arms tightly and kissing my head. "You'll do great and all the kids who benefit from this will forever thank you."

I nod into his chest, then shove him away when he undoes my bun and cackles. "River Jacobs!" I snap, though I can't help but laugh, too.

"Take it down. You aren't a stuffy old lady." He waggles his brows. "Yet."

"Go away." I wave him away and work on undoing the bun. As he makes his way down the stairs, I run my fingers through my red curls and stare at my reflection one last time. "We're gonna do this, and we're gonna do it right."

"Raven," Phoenix calls. "Don't make me come up there and bring you down. You won't like what happens later."

I'm tempted to skip the meeting entirely with those promises in the air.

"Not a *funishment*," he shouts again, as if he could hear my thoughts.

Snickering, I pull my jacket together and step into my flats. I hate the fact that I'm practically wearing a pantsuit, but I have to be presentable for a meeting with the mayor.

I grip the bannister firmly as I make my way down the stairs, with my eyes locked on Phoenix's warm gaze and tender smile.

Never have I felt so loved.

Even the best of Pierce's times, when he was adamant that the world revolved around me, pale in comparison to the overflow of love from all of them.

My heart hurts from what we've endured recently, but when River appears at the door and holds his hand out, I smile brightly. He and Phoenix escort me to the Jeep like the Queen they tell me I am.

"One last thing before we leave," Phoenix says. He turns me toward the open garage and I gasp.

There, looking fresh as the rest of us, is Pierce. Standing and smiling, without his crutches. We tossed most of his bandages days ago, leaving only bruises and a few scrapes behind, but I didn't think he'd be standing on his own again so soon.

"You're..." I stutter, tears threatening to fall. I have to hold them back to keep my makeup intact.

"Doc said I could toss the crutches this morning," he says, opening his arms wide.

I rush to hug him, but have to stop short of jumping into his arms. "I'm so glad!"

"If he gets dizzy, he has to sit down immediately," River chimes in. "The head injury really was the worst part of it."

"Swear the stitches are almost gone, though," Pierce grumbles.

"Can we go already?" Phoenix asks. "Being late to this meeting would look bad on all of us."

"Okay!" I turn around and rush toward the back door of the Jeep.

River opens it and lets me in before getting into the driver's seat, since Pierce was told no driving until his dizziness went away completely.

He grumbles about being driven around, but I think he secretly likes us having to cart him around.

"Speech prepared?" Phoenix asks as he slides into the seat next to me.

I nod and wring my hands together.

He grabs them in his and kisses my knuckles, with his gaze locked on mine. "It'll be fine, Red. You're going to help so many kids this way. You'll be making the world much, much better."

"I know, it's just—"

"Big and scary?" Pierce chimes in.

I nod.

"I'll show you something big and scary," River says, chuckling. He laughs harder when Pierce punches his shoulder and sighs.

"You're all incredibly childish," Phoenix grumbles, hiding his smile with a hand over his mouth.

It's not long before we're parking outside of the lot the community center used to sit on. They tore the building down a week ago. Apparently, the building was full of mold and other substances that meant it'd cost more to clean it than it would to rebuild the whole thing.

Now, I have to properly pitch this to Hargraves.

"You'll do great, Red," Phoenix says, helping me out of the Jeep. He kisses my forehead, then passes me to River, who gives me the same treatment and passes me to Pierce.

"Little bird," Pierce whispers, tilting my chin up so I meet his gaze. "This is what you were meant to do. I can feel it."

"I hope so. But what about you guys?"

His lips quirk into a grin as he pulls something from his pocket and holds it out to me.

I grab it and turn it over to reveal a business card showcasing the tire shop's logo with Hill's Auto plastered on the front. "B-But w-why—"

"Because," he says, "your parents deserved more than they got. We're building a legacy, and it's not on the names of shit humans."

"Hello?" Phoenix snaps.

"Excluding his parents, who were saints," Pierce says with a roll of his eyes. He leans down and kisses my nose before pulling back. "Now," he says, turning me around, "go pitch this to Hargraves and change some lives."

"You guys aren't coming with me?" I squeak, turning toward them in panic.

"You've got this, little vixen," River says. He grabs my shoulders and turns me back around. "Go. Kick ass." He slaps my ass and laughs when I jump.

"Men," I grumble, then straighten myself and walk to

the center of the lot where Hargraves is standing. "Mayor Hargraves."

"Please, call me Grayson," he says, holding out his hand.

"Sorry," I say, taking his hand. "Grayson. I'm really thankful you've asked to meet with me."

He grins and shoves his hands in his pockets. "Pitch it to me, Miss Hill."

I nod a few times. "Okay. So. I grew up here. In this town. Many kids ended up getting too bored because no one was really looking out for them. They were lost, estranged, neglected, betrayed, abused. Many are no longer with us, but to this day, Mr. Grayson, the impact of their youth is felt by many. With the community youth center, there will be a place for those lost, neglected, and abused kids to turn to. It will be a safe haven for all youth, no matter their life circumstances, to come and be themselves and get help if they need it, or silence if they want it." I take a deep breath and glance down at my feet before gathering the courage to meet his gaze. See his smile.

"What will you call it?"

"Well," I say, "it may be a little cheesy, but..." I take another deep breath and square my shoulders. "Raven's Nest."

He chuckles. "Well, Raven," he says, turning and looking over the now empty lot. "It seems we have a rather big nest to build here."

"Yes, we do."

"It's going to be a lot of work to maintain this."

"I'm ready for it."

"May take a year or two to get it up and running."

"That's fine. I need a breather after the last year of my life."

"Then it's yours."

"I totally—" I gape at him. "Wait, really?"

He nods. "What you're going to do for this community is too important to tell you no. This will change lives, Miss Hill, and those lives you change? They could change the world."

"I... I don't know what to say." I turn back to see the guys, but they're looking at something on a phone together. When I turn back toward Grayson, I point at the guys over my shoulder. "They have the blueprints."

"Mr. West sent them over this morning."

"Financial plans?"

"Also sent by Mr. West."

"Well, shit."

Chuckling, Grayson pulls out his ringing phone, then sighs and pockets it again. "I have some other things to handle, but I imagine we'll be seeing a lot of each other over the coming months and years."

Too stunned to speak, I watch as he walks to his SUV, gets in, and drives down Main Street. Then, as if in slow motion, I turn around and walk in a haze back to the guys.

As I get closer, Pierce shoves his phone in his pocket and they all stare at me, waiting expectantly.

"Well?" Phoenix asks.

"It's mine," I breathe.

"Fuck yes!" River shouts, lifting me in his arms and spinning me around. "I knew taking your hair down would help!"

I snort and shake my head. As he places me down, I hold on to his arms and look between all three of them. "We're finally making the world a place we want to live in."

"And it's all because of you, little bird."

"It's all because of us," I retort. "None of this would have been possible without all of you here to help along the way."

"Did more harm than good in the beginning though," River says.

I shrug. "Sometimes darkness, however necessary or unnecessary, leads us to the light we wouldn't have seen otherwise. And the light within my darkness?" I meet all of their gazes. "All of you."

"Aw shucks. You're making me blush!"

Phoenix sighs and pulls the Jeep door open. "Get in the damn car, River."

He does, and the rest of us follow suit.

Soon, we're heading home, with our pain far, far behind us, and a new horizon ready for us to build upon it.

## *raven*

## FOURTH OF JULY

"Phoenix motherfucking West!"

Phoenix grins and releases my hand as he crosses through the backyard toward a group of people standing near a small outdoor stage. He's wrapped up in hug after hug and swept into conversation almost immediately.

I lean against Pierce's shoulder and watch. "He needed this."

Pierce wraps his arm around my shoulders and kisses my head. "Definitely. We all needed a little getaway. Been too damn busy to take a decent break lately."

River saunters over with a plate piled to its limit with food. He shoves a pickle in his mouth, then hands a burger to Pierce and a hot dog to me. No choice given. We accept the food or it falls to our feet.

And I'm a fan of mine at the moment.

Yesterday, the boys sent me out on a spa day a town over, citing it as a birthday gift.

But something else is up, and my nerves are shot to shit.

"I need you to try one of these pickles," River says. He shoves one in my hand and I pull out of Pierce's embrace so I can hold it and my newly acquired hot dog.

"River," I chastise, "it's only been like two minutes. How did you end up with so much food already?"

"Easy, I told them my girlfriend was hangry." He takes a bite of his pickle and shrugs when I glare at him.

"You're annoying," Pierce grumbles, but he bites into his burger anyway.

We spend a few minutes stuffing our faces and watching Phoenix catch up with his old bandmates. The heat attempts to kill us all, but the promise of cooler weather in a few hours during the fireworks is enough to keep me going. That, and the bright smiles on my guys' faces.

"Hey, Red!" Phoenix shouts. "Get over here!"

I kiss Pierce's and River's cheeks, then make my way across the yard.

Phoenix pulls me into his side the moment I'm close enough, and starts pointing around at all the people, telling me their names. Ryan, Max, Owen, Rachel, and a few others linger around. He points out their parents in the background, and the missing hole his parents made up becomes a bit more obvious.

"They'd have been so proud of you, Nix," Ryan says, slapping him on the back. "A garage? This center your girl is putting together?"

"We're proud of you too, man," Owen, I think, says.

"Max and I were just talking about playing the song." Ryan grins. "I bet you haven't heard him really play, huh?"

I shake my head. "Not really. Here and there he plays the guitar when he thinks no one's listening. He sings while he cooks, but never loud enough to really appreciate."

"It's a life I left behind," Phoenix grumbles.

"Didn't have to," I say sincerely, turning to look up at him. "Still don't have to."

"I'm good where I'm at. Promise." He leans down and kisses me softly before turning toward his friends again. "I'll play it with you."

"Hell yeah!" Max pumps his fist into the air. He fist bumps Ryan, and they whisk Phoenix away with them. No doubt to get him set up.

Thirty minutes later, as more people fill the yard and my anxiety skyrockets, Pierce pulls me into his lap. He wraps his arms around me and leans back in the camping chair, and River sits in one next to us.

"You're gonna need a long nap after tonight," Pierce says, kissing my cheek.

"It's just…"

"A lot of people? I get it. I could feel you buzzing all the way across the yard, little bird." He tightens his hold around my waist and rests his chin on my shoulder. "We can go home whenever you want to."

I shake my head and look at the stage where Phoenix is smiling the biggest smile and cracking jokes with his old friends. "I don't want to take this moment away from him."

"Fair enough." With a soft kiss to the shell of my ear, Pierce drops the subject and rests his hands on my thighs as we watch the band finally take the stage.

"I'm so stoked," River says in between bites of chocolate cake.

Where he got it and how much he's already had is a mystery.

"Welcome to our humble abode," Ryan says, snickering when a woman sighs loudly from behind me. "Sorry.

Welcome to my mom's home. She's glad to have you here but wants you gone right after the fireworks are over so she can happily bang my dad."

"Ryan Lawson!" the woman snaps.

A man beside her chuckles and kisses her cheek as he pulls her into his lap, soothing her with soft touches.

"Anyway," Ryan drawls into the microphone, "we have Nix here to open this show up with us tonight." Turning, Ryan grins at Phoenix and points to him. "Phoenix West, welcome back, even if it's just for the next three minutes, brother."

Phoenix rolls his eyes and shakes his head before strumming on the guitar.

Goosebumps rise on my skin.

"We're starting out with a song most of you should have memorized by now," Ryan speaks into the mic.

The drummer picks up a soft beat.

"And if you don't, you're quickly going to learn," Ryan says while staring at Pierce, River, and me.

My heart hammers with the low strum of the bass line.

"This," Ryan says, holding the microphone between both hands and staring out at the small crowd, "is Phoenix Rising."

"THAT WAS SO FUCKING EPIC!" River says about an hour later.

Phoenix grins and wipes the sweat from his brow with the bottom of his shirt, revealing his deliciously tattooed abs. He winks when he catches me staring, then pulls me in for a hug and a quick kiss. "Sorry I played longer."

"Don't be sorry, Nix." I lean up on my toes and kiss him quickly, then grin at him. "It was amazing seeing you in your element like that."

He shrugs and goes in for another kiss.

Someone clears their throat, and we turn to see an older woman with tears in her gorgeous blue eyes.

"Mrs. Bishop," Phoenix says, releasing me in favor of pulling her in for a hug.

She stifles a sob and hugs him tight for a moment before pulling away and wiping her eyes. "They'd be so proud of you. Whatever you're doing right now, keep doing it. Sabrina would have been thrilled with how happy you are."

Phoenix nods and clears his throat a few times before trying to speak again. "Thank you so much, Mrs. Bishop. Really. Means a lot coming from you."

Turning toward me, she looks me over, then smiles brightly and pulls me in for a hug. "Thank you for loving our little Nixy."

Phoenix groans when I laugh at the name. "Don't even," he says, probably in warning to River.

"Wouldn't dream of it," River blatantly lies.

Pulling back, she smiles at me and looks between my men and I. "More power to you for putting up with three. I can barely put up with the one."

"I take offense to that, Angel." A man, I think Phoenix said his name was Ryan, pulls the woman into his arms. "You did good out there, Nix."

"Thank you, Mr. Bishop."

"Am I really that stuffy that everyone thinks I want to be called mister anything?" He looks at his wife. "Really?"

She pats his chest and snickers. "Absolutely. You've been that stuffy since we met. Come on. Let's give the kids some space before the fireworks begin." Turning toward us again, she smiles. "Have fun!"

"She's funny," I tell Phoenix as he pulls me into his arms.

"Speaking of fireworks," Pierce says, meeting the other guys' gazes before locking eyes with me. "We have a little surprise for you."

"What—" I try to ask what type of surprise, but Phoenix tosses a blindfold over my eyes and all three guys work together to escort me to who knows where.

It's as if a century goes by before they finally slow down and let go of me.

The air surrounding me goes cold the moment they step away.

"What the hell are you doing?" I ask.

"Remove the blindfold, Red."

Shakily, because I can feel what's happening, I do as I'm told.

In front of me, on bended knee, are all three of my men. A backdrop of the moon and stars behind them, and a blanket with enough pillows and snacks to keep us comfortable through the rest of the night.

"Guys, I—"

"Little vixen," River begins, "I fell in love with you the moment you let me take you shopping and steal a kiss from you. When I saw your carefree spirit try to come out and play despite all the bullshit we were doing to you? I knew I wanted to be by your side for however long you'd let me."

"Riv—"

"Raven," Phoenix says. He swallows harshly, then meets my eyes. "I know when we met in therapy, it wasn't supposed to be a place to connect. And I know I lied by not telling you it was me in those emails, but you showed me your soul so early on, and truly, that was the moment I fell in love. It was only after seeing your strength this past year that I knew what it meant to want to be with someone forever."

"Nix—"

Pierce takes a deep breath and locks his eyes on mine, getting lost in my sea of blue as much as I've always gotten lost in the green forest in his. "Blue, you've been everything to me since we were eight years old. We planned a whole wedding out before we ever knew what it really meant to be married. Adding these two to the mix will only enhance the love I give you. While I've treated you like hell, and you've forgiven me, I'll still spend the rest of our lives apologizing to you. Marry us, little bird? Let us give you forever?"

Tears stream down my face, and snot threatens to make this a pure, ugly cry. But a week ago, when I found the gorgeous black diamond ring sitting on the bedside table, I already had my answer. I already knew what I wanted to do.

"N-No," I stutter out.

"The fuck do you mean no?" Pierce asks, panic evident in his voice.

"Did we do something wrong?" Phoenix asks, tilting his head in confusion.

"We haven't given you enough orgasms over the last week, right? Is that it?"

"River!" Pierce, Phoenix, and I shout in unison.

He shrugs. "Only trying to troubleshoot here."

"It's not a no forever," I tell them, meeting each of their gazes. "It's a no for right now."

"Why?" Pierce asks.

"Because we've been through hell and back and I'm completely fine with how things are right now. There's no need for a big wedding or marriage or b—"

"Babies?" River asks, perking up a little.

"Exactly." I sigh and take a step forward. I place my hands on either side of Pierce's dejected face and kiss his forehead before standing straight. "I want to live a little before we do this."

"So... it's not a no forever, but a not right now?" he asks.

I nod.

"So if I ask you to wear the ring as a promise, so I know you aren't going to leave us anytime soon, you'd do it?"

I raise a brow.

"He wants to mark you publicly, Red," Phoenix says. "We all do."

I sigh and hold out my left hand, placing my right on my hip as I give them all the sass I have left in me today. "You're neanderthals."

Pierce happily shoves the ring onto my finger, then lifts me into the air. "She said yes!" he bellows into the night air, as fireworks boom and sizzle above us.

"I said later!" I shout back at him.

He grins and shrugs. "Later is better than never, Blue."

"This way," River says, "we can have all the time to practice for babies, too."

"Oh my god," I groan, pressing my forehead onto Pierce's shoulder.

"Think of all the orgasms between now and later, Red," Phoenix says in my ear.

"And all the ways we can spoil you," Pierce adds.

"Okay, okay," I say, giggling. "Let's just enjoy the here and now. When I'm ready–truly ready–I'll let you know."

We lay out with our snacks and watch the sky above us explode into fountains of color, surrounded by love, happiness, and the promise of our future wrapped snugly around my finger.

**THE END**

**But if you need more and you want to read the bonus epilogue set 5 years in the future head over to** https://authorshelbylee.com/RNBonus

THANK you so much for reading Raven's Nest! I would absolutely love it if you wrote a review to help spread the word. Even if you hated it.

For all updates on my books, deleted scenes, short stories, early access, teasers, and even more shenanigans, come join the Dark & Twisted Library at https://reamstories.com/authorshelbylee

## *acknowledgments*

We're sticking with 'this book was different' from River Run's massive word count difference between Pierce Me and Phoenix Flames.

I have found my fucking voice. Finally.

It's been a struggle between expectations, reality, and neurodivergent bullshit, but I finally have.

I'm so proud of this series, and I can't wait to continue on this journey with you, dear reader.

I really want to thank you for being here and reading all of this series. It's my first, and it's finally completed. It means a lot to me to have this finished, and even more that you're HERE... in this moment... on this page.

Thank you, thank you, thank you.

To Kennedy... thank you for always being a great support, through tears and rants and all of my changes to this point. You've been a glowing star for me, and I'm so grateful I get to call you a friend.

To Drea, Kendall & Sylvia... MDCS... y'all are the goddamn best and will forever be stuck with me. I'm not even sorry. Thank you for the support through this series and for becoming some amazing readers-turned-friends.

Thank you to my Visitor's Pass & Library Cardholders in the Dark & Twisted Library... you guys help me continue on this journey with each new month you're a member.

Thank you to my VIP Cardholders: Drea, Kendall, Sylvia, Tori, Kat, Kelly, Jennifer & Brandi. You are such amazing supporters and I'll forever be grateful for you.

A huge shoutout to Bug & Bubba. I have had a blast bouncing ideas off of you two, even if you can't read the books you help me create yet.

And lastly, to my husband, for being the absolute amazing support system and sounding board. My accountant, shipping person, motivator, and absolute love of my life. This entire series is only possible because of your love for me, and I feel it every single day I wake up and realize I'm living my actual dream. Thank you.

Okay. I'll get off my soapbox now.

Now on to the next series, The Tragedies that Bind Us, which will follow Xavier Hayes, someone we only slightly know, and someone we haven't yet met. It's going to be dark, dirty, and an absolute blast. ;)

Sincerely,

Shelby Lee

# also by shelby lee

**A Conspiracy of Ravens**

1. Pierce Me

2. Phoenix Flames

3. River Run

4. Raven's Nest

**The Tragedies that Bind Us**

0.5 Overnight (An ACoR Spin-Off Novella)

1. Unforgotten

Want to read all of Shelby Lee's books for one price? Join The Dark & Twisted Library at https://reamstories.com/authorshelbylee & instantly gain access to all stories, a community of other Dark & Twisted Readers and more!

Shelby Lee is a neurospicy author who writes books that tear people apart before putting them back together again - with anywhere from a dash to a whole serving of spice.

Her stories vary in shades of darkness. Sometimes the books are nearing rom-com status with dark themes, and other times... well... she hits the abyss. She's creating a universe full of characters she hopes you'll like, loathe, and love.

She lives in the middle of the United States with her husband and kids and can be found gaming or binging tv shows when she isn't reading or writing.

You'll most likely find her on Ream inside of the Dark & Twisted Library at https://reamstories.com/authorshelbylee sharing extra snippets, phone wallpapers, along with writing and life updates.

www.ingramcontent.com/pod-product-compliance
Lightning Source LLC
Chambersburg PA
CBHW070506300726
48975CB00007B/2338